THE LANCASHIRE STRING BAND

Gardner's Family Band
(St Helens), *c.*1880.

The Lancashire String Band

Social dance musicians in the county, 1880–1930

David Middlehurst

Dedicated to my father, Philip Middlehurst

www.facebook.com/pages/The-Lancashire-String-Band
d.middlehurst@btinternet.com

First published in 2015 on behalf of the author by
Scotforth Books (www.scotforthbooks.com)

ISBN: 978-1-909817-26-5

Typesetting and design by Carnegie Book Production, Lancaster
Printed in the UK by Print-On-Demand Worldwide, Peterborough

Contents

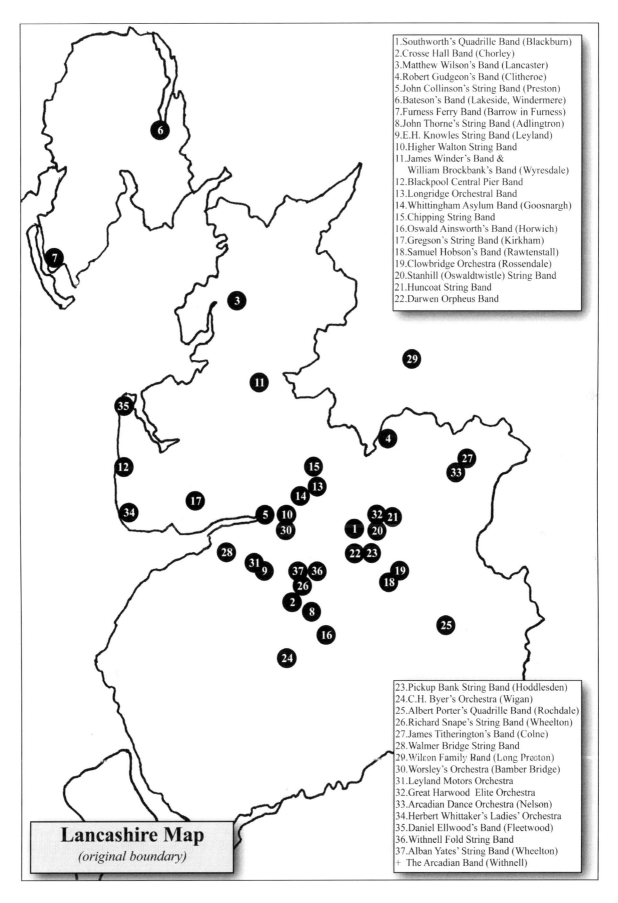

Lancashire Map
(original boundary)

1. Southworth's Quadrille Band (Blackburn)
2. Crosse Hall Band (Chorley)
3. Matthew Wilson's Band (Lancaster)
4. Robert Gudgeon's Band (Clitheroe)
5. John Collinson's String Band (Preston)
6. Bateson's Band (Lakeside, Windermere)
7. Furness Ferry Band (Barrow in Furness)
8. John Thorne's String Band (Adlingtron)
9. E.H. Knowles String Band (Leyland)
10. Higher Walton String Band
11. James Winder's Band &
    William Brockbank's Band (Wyresdale)
12. Blackpool Central Pier Band
13. Longridge Orchestral Band
14. Whittingham Asylum Band (Goosnargh)
15. Chipping String Band
16. Oswald Ainsworth's Band (Horwich)
17. Gregson's String Band (Kirkham)
18. Samuel Hobson's Band (Rawtenstall)
19. Clowbridge Orchestra (Rossendale)
20. Stanhill (Oswaldtwistle) String Band
21. Huncoat String Band
22. Darwen Orpheus Band

23. Pickup Bank String Band (Hoddlesden)
24. C.H. Byer's Orchestra (Wigan)
25. Albert Porter's Quadrille Band (Rochdale)
26. Richard Snape's String Band (Wheelton)
27. James Titherington's Band (Colne)
28. Walmer Bridge String Band
29. Wilson Family Band (Long Preston)
30. Worsley's Orchestra (Bamber Bridge)
31. Leyland Motors Orchestra
32. Great Harwood Elite Orchestra
33. Arcadian Dance Orchestra (Nelson)
34. Herbert Whittaker's Ladies' Orchestra
35. Daniel Ellwood's Band (Fleetwood)
36. Withnell Fold String Band
37. Alban Yates' String Band (Wheelton)
+ The Arcadian Band (Withnell)

Oswaldtwistle musicians.

Preface

THE PURCHASE of an old postcard from a local antique fair provided the background for this book. The photograph included five musicians and a sheet of piano music with the words 'The Lancers' on the front cover, indicating that this was a dance band. On the reverse was written simply 'A Chorley Band'.

My curiosity led me to visit Chorley Library, in the hope of finding some more information about this intriguing image. I estimated that the photograph must have been taken just prior to the First World War and I initially began to search through local newspapers to identify the character of social activity across communities during this period.

'A Chorley Band' – the postcard that sparked my initial interest.

The acquisition of more photographs, primarily in the Lancashire area, meant that I could then visit libraries in other parts of the county to try and build a picture of the social role of these types of bands. Matching newspaper articles to the band photographs proved to be quite a difficult but extremely rewarding task.

A large amount of information in this book is recorded in the form of snippets gleaned from local Lancashire newspapers between 1880 and the 1920s and many of those are extracts from reports published in the *Preston Guardian*. It should be pointed out that the circulation of this publication covered virtually the whole county at that time, so that reports from places as far apart as the Lake District, Lancaster, Clitheroe, Colne and Preston, for instance, would regularly appear together in the same issue. There were no localised editions for specific areas, rather 'District News' sections in the same issue. Similarly, when the same event has been reported in more than one publication, it is the *Preston Guardian* report that has generally been the chosen text.

There is a surprising amount of detail in the newspapers and it was evident that most villages, had their own string band and they played a large part in the social life of their respective communities.

The articles also provided information about instruments used and music played. They record the locations where the dances took place and reveal what times of year were the most popular for these events. Included also are some references to other related bands providing music for dancing.

I was very fortunate in being able to meet relatives and descendants of some of the musicians and record more personal family detail from them. The information they gave would never have been available from other sources and my gratitude to them is immense.

David Middlehurst, June 2015

Music and dance

THE START of the nineteenth century saw an influx of new fashionable dances from Europe and they quickly spread from the formal balls in the large towns to small village events throughout Lancashire. Reports in the Lancashire newspapers sometimes gave a detailed account of the dances that took place.

In Preston on 11 January 1845: 'St Augustine's Ball, which was held on Monday last, in the upper room of St Augustine's School, was attended by a gay and numerous assembly. About eight o'clock, the musicians, Westby's Polka and Quadrille Band, took their places in an orchestra at one end of the apartment, to a "concord of sweet sounds", with a country dance. The quadrille succeeded quadrille, diversified occasionally with the rustic dance.'

There was a resistance to the new fashions as this account from Goosnargh shows. On 17 May 1845: 'There were the usual attractions of a well conducted village fair and with these the company heartily enjoyed themselves. In the evening the fiddles were called into requisition for the votaries of dancing. Polkas, Mazurkas, and Lancers found no favourites; country dances, jigs and reels were preferred, and the merry swains and pretty damsels of Goosnargh, tript it gaily.' A similar sentiment was also expressed in an article from Preston on 24 December 1846: 'On Saturday evening last, a Tea Party was held at Mr Hood's Temperance Hotel, Lune Street.' After the presentation, 'The fiddles were called into requisition and dancing became the order of the evening'. 'Mazourkas, waltzes, and the "fascinating polka", seemed to find no favour in the eyes of the fair damsels constituting the company, but gave place to "Sir Roger de Coverley", "Scotch reels", and Quadrilles, which kept up with increasing spirit for some time.'

In Preston on 15 January 1862: 'The annual Oddfellow's Ball was held at The Exchange Rooms on Monday evening. They commenced the evening's enjoyment with the country dance, to the inspiring strains of Mr Catterall's Quadrille Band, which gave very great satisfaction. The following music was performed to the various dances allotted: Quadrilles; Off to Charleston, Erin-go-Bragh, Empress, Juno by Farmer, Dixy's Land (Catterall), My Mary Ann. Lancers; Original, The New Lancers (D'Albert), Royal Lancers, Montrose, The New Lancers (Catterall). Waltzes: Wild Buds (Masson), Nelly Gray (D'Albert), Songs of the Wood (Coote), Geraldene (Masson), Gallops; Dixy's, Rifleman (Tinney). Varsoviannas; Silver Lake (Montgomery), Golden Stream. Schottisches; Atlantic, Rainbow, Red Scar (Catterall). Polkas; Kiss Me Quick, &c.'

Quadrille Bands were able to adapt to the occasion, as this report in Preston on 21 March 1874 shows: 'St Patrick's Day was celebrated in the Assembly Rooms of the Corn Exchange. The portrait paintings of Daniel O'Connell and Thomas Francis Maher (the American General) were suspended at the north and south ends of the room. Mr. Willacy's Quadrille Band occupied the orchestra and with its spirited strains the dance was thoroughly enjoyed. Some of the dance music was adapted to Irish airs and this of course met with especial approval. "The Irish reel" and the "Irish jig", which were introduced, seemed to draw all true Irishmen to their legs.'

A fund-raising Tea Party and Ball was held in Leyland on 31 January 1885. The event took place at the Railway and Commercial Hotel and 400 people were present. Mr Collinson's String Band from Preston played for the ball and the report informs us that the band was 'greatly augmented', presumably because of the size of the event. It is interesting to note that a list of all the dances is included in the article and the repertoire is the same as the one for the Quadrille Bands. The first dance was a country dance followed by a selection of dances including polkas, quadrilles, polka mazurkas, waltzes, schottishes, mazurkas, lancers, varsoviennas, gallops and finishing with Sir Roger de Coverley. 'Joseph Cross performed the duties of Master of Ceremonies.'

Dances were often the main social event of the week and dancing lessons were seen as important. The following account is an extract from an eighty seven year old lady from Morecambe: 'I was born at Pole Lane, Darwen, and in 1896, aged 17, I was a cotton weaver in a local mill. I was learning to dance. It cost 6d. and 1d. for the concertina player. We had sixpenny dances at the Sunday School.'[1]

At Halton, near Lancaster, on 3 January 1903: 'A social was held in the National Schoolroom in connection with the select dancing class. A first class programme was discoursed by Mr W.A. Willis's Dance Band. Mr Willis, teacher of the class acted as MC.'

As late as 1904, classes for quadrille were mentioned. On 9 January:

'QUADRILLE CLASS – On New Year's Day, an invitation dance was held in the Carnforth Co-operative Hall in connection with Mr P.G. Dance's Quadrille Class. About 100 were present. During the evening an exhibition dance was rendered by eight children who had specially trained for the occasion. The music was supplied by Mr Winder of Lancaster.'

The following is an account of the Preston Farmers' Ball at the Public Hall dated 23 January 1909: 'On Tuesday, Preston was the mecca for every farmer's son and daughter, for miles around. The two-step, the old-fashioned schottische and the Valeta were very popular.'

'In the olden days, dancing was taught in the country. There was formerly an old fiddler near Garstang who taught the schottische in a very curious fashion. This was his style: "Neaw lads and lasses. Ger at it. On yer reet is t'cupboard door, on your left an owd settee. Them's yer landmarks. Neaw altogether, one to th' cupboard shuffle, shuffle one to th'owd settee shuffle shuffle; one on, two on, three, four and so on." And I am told that he made very good dancers.'

Bands would also provide dancing lessons. In October 1912 the *Preston Guardian* reported that 'Dancing classes were formed at the Longridge Co-operative Hall under the auspice of Longridge Orchestral Band. There was a large turn out on Thursday night.'

Children were taught to dance and would be expected to take part in various events as in this example from Longridge: 'A children's carnival was organised by the Longridge Branch of the Fylde and District Women's Constitutional Association in the Co-operative Hall. The event commenced with the dancing of a polka, to a medley of John Peel. In all, about 300 children of all denominations from Longridge and district took part. After dancing the Valeta and the Barn dance, the next item was crowning the May Queen.'

Dancing masters visited villages in Lancashire to teach children the various dances. On 4 January 1908 the *Lancaster Guardian* reports that 'The pupils of Mr Jos. Robinson held their first Ball in the Assembly Room at the Royal Hotel, Burton in Kendal, on Tuesday. A very interesting programme, including clog, hornpipe, reel, tambourine and

String band music, 1908.

other dances, was gone through.' Jos. Robinson had been a well-known dancing master in the north Lancashire and Lakes area and his brother Alf taught dancing between Lancaster and Kendal right up to 1928.[2]

Sheet music for the string bands could be obtained from the local music shop. The illustration (*page 3*) is the front cover of a first violin part for string band concert music. There are also examples of sheet music for dancing, often with newly composed tunes.

At the top of the front cover is stamped 'Haigh String Band'. Haigh is a small mining village to the north-west of the Wigan. There is a reference to the band in the Horwich Chronicle on 9 February 1907: 'There was a tea and social gathering promoted by the Young Women's class of the Blackrod Parish Church in the school rooms on Saturday evening. The Haigh String Band provided the music for dancing.'

Church bands

VILLAGE MUSICIANS often had a dual role, playing music to accompany Sunday service and also providing dance music. There are two well-documented examples in Lancashire.

The 'Shepherd's Church', Over Wyresdale, lies near Abbeystead in the Forest of Bowland. The vestry in the church contains instruments that were used by village musicians, both to accompany the congregation in church and also to play for local dances. They include clarinets, a cello, flutes and a bassoon. The Winder family had been connected with the church for generations and they were also involved in the music of the local villages. A number of musical manuscripts belonging to members of the family survive to this day and contain examples of dance tunes and religious music, often in the same book.

Goodshaw Chapel lies on a hillside in Rossendale, between Rawtenstall and Burnley. The area was well known for its musicians, who locally became known as ''Th' Deighn Layrocks' or the 'Larks o' Dean'.[3]

The singing in the Goodshaw chapel was accompanied by musical instruments. Some of the instruments were made by the musicians themselves and are on display in Rossendale Museum; the cello and fiddle certainly look homemade. There are also two clarinets and a serpent in the display case.[4] As well as accompanying singing in the chapel, the James Nuttall music manuscripts show that they also played for dancing.[5]

An interesting article by Samuel Compston, in the *Rossendale Free Press* of 12 November 1904, provides information about the Larks of Dean. He interviewed Moses Heap, a former member of the 'Layrocks', and Moses stated that there had been a quadrille band formed by members of the Larks of Dean. He knew that 'cello player Robert Ashworth had been in the band and that they took their practising seriously. 'A String Band under Robert o't' Carr was composed. I learned through Mr Richard Hargreaves, of James Ashworth, first violin; his father [old Robert] second violin; Jimmy o't' Parsons and John Hargreaves, violincello and Richard himself with trombone or violin as occasion required.'

Richard Hargreaves spent much time at the home of Jimmy o't' Parsons, or Jimmy o't' James, where they constantly played music. Among their possessions was a small hand written book containing many old tunes, including 'A lesson by Mr Handel', 'Come Haste to the Wedding', 'Buttered Peas', 'Stanley for ever', 'The Foxhunter's Jig', 'The Duke's March', 'Young Pattywack', 'Jig by Doctor Green' and 'Britton's Glory' (*sic*).

There is also evidence of musicians in other Lancashire churches. Hoghton parish church, between Preston and Blackburn, provides some information about instruments in the church: 'Thomas Miller was born in 1840 at Vale House, Hoghton Bottoms.' In 1885 he recorded that 'the choir was on the south side of the free seats. Robert Baron played an instrument with a crooked end and about four feet long [a bassoon]. Jonathan Smith, a hunchback, played a bass fiddle. There were other instrumentalists, including a fiddler and a clarinet player. An organ was introduced in 1868 which replaced the church band of musicians. More recently, Mrs Waring of Riley Green gave to Miss J. Wadsworth an antique bassoon that had originally been played in the church by musician Mr Smith.' The instrument was returned to the church and is now displayed on the west wall.[6]

This article in the *Preston Guardian* of 2 September 1871 shows what the author felt about the introduction of the organ into the service at his church in Poulton-le-Fylde, near Blackpool. It describes the singing in 1871 'as if the members of the choir were frightened and needed a sudden nipping, or hitting or frightening to stir them into life and make them shout out; the playing on the organ (bought in 1855 at a cost of £205), was, considering the instrument, tastefully executed. We, however, hardly know whether the performances of this choir were superior to those of olden times, for in days gone by matters were very lively in the music pew. There were in it men and women who sung lustily; there were clarinet, fiddle and bassoon players in it and if there was not much melody, there was a preponderance of what the present choir lacks – vigour and variety.'

In the *Blackburn Standard* of 30 October 1886: 'DEATH OF AN OLD MUSICIAN – Mr Thomas Higson, an old and familiar form in the village of Downham, died at home on Saturday afternoon. Deceased had attained his 70th year and was well known in the district. He had been leader of the Downham Parish Church for a period of about 50 years and had played the bass fiddle there during that time.'

In the *Preston Guardian* of 2 February 1895: 'The death of Chipping Octogenarian, Mr Henry Handley, was reported at the age of 87. As a musical man he had few equals, the violin, flute and clarinet being his favourite instruments. For many years he had also played the bass fiddle in the Chipping Parish Church.' In the same newspaper on 23 March 1895: 'An old musical instrument was found at Chipping, a violincello that had done service in the Chipping Parish Church before the organ was installed.'

The *Lancashire Evening Post* of 27 December 1933 printed an article entitled 'Lost in Snow with Bass Fiddle – Carol Singing 60 years ago.'

'Thomas Nowell Livesey of Tulketh Road, Preston, now 76 and born in 1857, had grown up in the village of Mitton in the Ribble Valley. He had been involved with music from an early age and had started singing carols when ten years old. His father was organist, choirmaster and sexton at Mitton Parish Church.'

'He was the only boy in the band of carollers, and two or three fiddles and a cello accompanied them. Although they did not perform on Christmas Eve, they were out singing in the snow for days before and after

'Church Musicians' by Charles Green.

Christmas. They would set off early on Christmas morning and the first stop was at the vicarage where there was a breakfast waiting for them. Afterwards they went through the village singing and then had a second breakfast at The Three Fishes Inn.'

'In the evening they would visit other nearby villages and hamlets, Bashall Eves, Browsholme and Whitewell. One time I remember having to carry the bass fiddle because old Joe had been participating in too much of the hospitality. As I climbed a style Joe lurched into me and I fell headlong into a deep drift with the fiddle on top of me. When they eventually dragged me out I was still clutching the bass fiddle.'

'On several occasions Mr Livesey's little band was invited to play at the big mansions of the district; Dinckley Hall, on the side of the Hodder near Stonyhurst, Browsholme Hall, Standen Hall and Mitton Hall near Whalley.'

'Sometimes they would clear the servant's hall and the fiddlers would play for dancing. The squire, his wife, the visitors, the servants and the band would take part in the festivities. The dances carried on until the morning and I can well remember my father, who was the lead fiddler, playing "Sir Roger de Coverley" when he was fast asleep.'

The Black Pudding Band

THIS ARTICLE is from the *Accrington Observer and Times* in 1903. The churches mentioned in the article are in the Holden Wood and Hutch Bank areas of Haslingden in the Rossendale Valley.

'This band of local musicians, consisting of members of the choir from both the Primitive Methodists and the United Methodists (Salem) was formed in 1848 or 1850, the leader being Robert Brierley who played a clarinet. This instrument is defined in Collins' *Dictionary* as "a musical wind instrument of the reed kind; the leading instrument in a military band".'

'There were at least four more clarinet players – William Henry Rishton, John Rishton, Richard Barnes (Dicky Brush) and Ainsworth Elton. Two brothers, Richard and Thomas Barnes, sons of a Hutch Bank farmer and known as Dicky o' Dick's and Thomas o' Dicky's, both played the curious instrument known as the serpent or "black puddings" because of their extraordinary shape and jet-black colour. Billy o' Tets, whose real name I do not know, also played one of these instruments and the fourth was in the hands of a resident of Haslingden Grane, but I do not know his name.'

'Richard Hoyle, father of John Hoyle, played a French trumpet, a brass instrument with three flat keys about the size of a half-crown, whilst Robert Heap (Bob o' Sol's) played an ophicleide, a many-keyed instrument. John Rhebanks Green (father of John Singleton Green, late borough surveyor) played a bassoon, a reed instrument of wood, something like a chair leg (and this is what it is called).'

'These men were all enthusiastic musicians and we always thought it a great treat to listen to the band when they played for the Sunday School procession, or when they accompanied the congregation to the open air camp meetings, which were so popular during the 60s of the last century. I have listened to them at Christmas, when they were playing Christmas carols, when there was something most peculiarly sweet in these most curious of instruments. They appeared to be something indescribable but most pleasing in their wonderful music, which added a delicious charm which no brass band has ever yet approached. Perhaps it was only childish fancy, but I would like to obtain the opinion of others who remember them.'

'At the annual sermons and on other occasions at both chapels, the orchestra was augmented by at least three double bass instruments, in the capable hands of John Hoyle, John Collinge and Caleb Greenwood and a single bass fiddle was in the hands of James Warburton. Other instrumentalists I think took part in those most interesting musical treats. Even after the organ was put in the chapel, the band took part in the musical part of the service.'

A selection of dance bands

My intention was to concentrate on dance bands between the 1880s and 1930s. I also decided to collect information about social dancing and dance musicians from the earlier part of the nineteenth century to provide a background.

I have chosen the county of Lancashire with its original boundaries at the time these bands were playing. It is quite possible that the information will be broadly similar to that from many English counties.

The bands are placed in their approximate chronological order. Of course, some bands were in existence over a longer period of time and, in the case of some family bands, they continued in some form until the

late 1940s. I have collected information about many bands within the county and have chosen a selection of mainly village bands and orchestras, although there are some examples of bands from the larger towns in Lancashire.

Early nineteenth-century dance bands in Lancashire

For the formal occasions and Grand Balls, a group of musicians playing for dances was often termed a quadrille band. The quadrille, the waltz, the polka and other new dances were introduced into Britain from the Continent at the beginning of the nineteenth century and soon became fashionable.

Horabin's Quadrille Band from Manchester was very popular and there are many references to the band as they played at various prestigious events across northern England and North Wales. In the 1837 *Commercial Directory* of Manchester, Thomas Horabin is listed as a harpist, living at 14 Gartside Street in the city.

An account in the *Preston Chronicle* of 24 December 1831 reports that they played at a series of four assemblies at the Corn Exchange, Lune Street, Preston. The personnel of the band were 'Messrs Horabin playing first and second violins, harp and flagolet. The clarionet was played by Mr Johnson, first horn by Mr Hogg, second horn by Mr Parker, violincello by Mr Smith and double-bass by Mr Shorrock.'

A report, also in the *Preston Chronicle*, on 2 January 1839, shows that they played for a fund-raising ball in Chorley. 'The Ball took place at the Royal Oak Inn, for the benefit of the Chorley Dispensary, which was numerously and fashionably attended. Mr Horabin's Quadrille Band was in attendance and played admirably.'

One of the largest established balls in Preston was the Horse Fair Ball, held at the beginning of January in the Assembly Room of the Bull Inn, Church Street. Horabin's Quadrille Band played at most of these balls until this article of January 1st 1848, reported the event's demise: 'The Horse Fair Ball, that has for many years been the annual resort of the aristocratical families of the neighbourhood and the higher classes of the town, is discontinued.'

Advertisement in the *Preston Chronicle*, December 1841.

Similar bands became established in the north-west of England. Joseph Haslam's Quadrille Band from Preston played at many events in Lancashire. The *Preston Guardian*, on 8 November 1851, reported 'CATHOLIC TEA PARTY AND BALL – On Monday evening last a Tea Party and Ball, for the purpose of aiding the erection of the tower and spire of St Walburge's Church, Preston, took place in the Exchange Rooms in the town. There were about 900 in attendance including the leading Catholics in the town. After tea the company engaged in a dance to the strains of Haslam's Quadrille Band.'

Jasper Norwood (1824–98) was from a military background and was the bandmaster of the Preston Rifle Volunteers. He was a respected figure in Preston and other local Lancashire towns. The first reference to his band was on 12 August 1854 when they played for a dance at the Preston Regatta. 'A Ball got up by the Regatta committee was held in the Exchange Rooms last evening. The attendance was much more numerous than expected, August scarcely being the month for dancing; but the meeting was of a most agreeable character, and passed off well. Norwood's Band played most proficiently.'

Although most of their engagements were in Preston, the band played at events in nearby towns and villages. In Walton-le-Dale, on 30 August 1856, they played at a fund-raising event for the erection of a new Catholic Church. 'On Monday evening last, a Ball was held in Mr Richardson's corn mill, Walton-le-Dale, at which 600 persons were present, more indeed, than could comfortably dance. Norwood's Quadrille Band was in attendance and dancing was kept up until three o'clock.'

Advertisement in the *Preston Guardian*, July 1854.

Southworth's Quadrille Band (Blackburn)

MR BALDERSTONE was a highly regarded dance teacher in Blackburn, where he taught both junior and senior classes. The *Blackburn Standard* of 9 March 1837 had a report about one of his organised dances. 'On Friday evening the adult pupils of Mr Balderstone, the respected professor of dancing, gave a Ball at the New Inn at which about thirty couples were present. In the course of the evening a very handsome violin bow by Dodd, with a suitable inscription, was presented to Mr Balderstone.'

Two years later, on 20 March 1839, appeared the first reference to the Southworth Family Band, when they played at Mr Balderstone's Annual Victoria Ball at the New Inn. 'Mr Southworth's Quadrille band was engaged for the occasion and they acquitted themselves with great credit. The Quadrille, the stately Lancer, the military Mazourka and the homely Old English country dance, succeeded each other in rapid succession. The dancing closed with the last new and popular dance called The Circassian Circle.'

The instrumentalists of the band were named when they appeared in Walton-le-Dale on 30 September 1843: 'A band of music from Blackburn, known by the name of "Southworth's Family

Advertisement from the *Blackburn Standard.*

BRINDLE BALL.

THE Eighteenth Annual BALL, in aid of the funds of the School, will be held in the School Rooms, on MONDAY, JANUARY 6TH, 1851.

STEWARDS:

Mr. H. AINSWORTH.	Mr. R. COUPE.
Mr. R. BRIERLEY.	Mr. J. KENYON.
Mr. P. AINSWORTH.	Mr. M. MOTLER.
Mr. R. H. LATHAM.	Mr. J. WORSLEY.

Lady's Tickets, 2s. 6d.; Gentlemen's Tickets, 3s. 0d.; to be had at the *Guardian* and *Chronicle* Offices, and at Mrs. THOMSON's, Preston; *Standard* Office, Blackburn; and of the Stewards.

Southworth's Family Quadrille Band will be in attendance. Dancing to commence at Nine o'Clock.

The Evening Railway Trains from Preston and Blackburn will stop at the Bridge, near to the Schools.

JOHN Mc. MANUS, HON. SECTY.

Brindle, December 24th, 1850.

This advertisement is from the *Preston Guardian*. It is interesting to note that the train 'will stop at the Bridge, near to the Schools'.

Quadrille Band", consisting of father, son, and two daughters [one of the two daughters played on the harp, the other on the viol de gambo], enlivened the company and added to the gaiety of the occasion. They were assisted by Mr Jackson, a performer on the violin.'

Southworth's Quadrille Band played for the Oddfellows' Ball at the Black Horse Inn, Blackburn, on 29 August 1846. 'After some excellent speeches, the company formed for dancing. The services of Southworth's Band were called into requisition.'

The following year, they played at the Blackburn Mechanics' Institution at the Assembly Rooms, Heaton Street, Blackburn, 'The tables were cleared and Southworth's Band being again summoned to the orchestra, country dances, quadrilles, the lancers, the polka, cellarius and gallopedes followed in quick succession.'

In January 1850 and 1851, they played at the Annual Brindle Ball, near Chorley. The event took place in the Catholic School Room, Brindle. 'There was a large attendance, including visitors from Preston and Blackburn.' In

1850 they also played for Catholic balls at St Mary's in Blackburn and St Mary's in Burnley.

Celebrations at Whalley were recorded on 20 June 1850, when a special train was commissioned to carry civic dignities across the rebuilt Whalley Viaduct. 'On returning to Whalley, the party was again entertained in a huge marquee, erected in a field close to the station. Southworth's Quadrille Band played for dancing and the Whalley Glee Singers entertained from their extensive repertoire.'

In Blackburn, on 16 August 1851, the band was reported playing for the United Smiths' Sick Society. 'The society celebrated its anniversary on Monday last, at the Oak Inn, Blackburn, on which occasion fifty members and their wives sat down to an excellent dinner, after which Southworth's Quadrille Band was called into requisition.'

The band played for an Oddfellows' Ball and Soiree at the New Bull Inn, Church Street, Blackburn, in January 1856. In July 1859 they played at the Town Hall Assembly Room, Blackburn. 'Southworth's Quadrille Band played and dancing was kept up with "great spirit" until 2 o'clock in the morning.'

Finally, this time during January 1861, they appeared at the Clitheroe Volunteer Ball at the Assembly Rooms, Castle Street, Clitheroe.

Crosse Hall Band (Chorley)

THE Crosse Hall Printworks was housed in a mill building on the east side of Blackbrook, bordering the Leeds/Liverpool canal in Chorley. It re-opened in 1839 under the management of Richard Cobden, who had been involved with calico printing since the 1820s. Cobden was a man with a keen social awareness and was involved with the Anti-Corn Law League.

Richard Cobden's reputation as an employer was exceptional and he was described as generous and liberal. When the corn-laws were repealed, the workers at the mill celebrated the event in style.[7]

All references to the Crosse Hall Band are taken from the *Preston Guardian*. From 18 July 1846: 'The work's band headed a procession through Chorley's streets and lanes on Wednesday morning last. The whole of the persons – men, women and children, in the employ of R. Cobden Esq. MP at Crosse Hall print-works were treated with a trip to Fleetwood by their spirited employer, together with their wives. They paraded the town with two bands and a large assortment of banners. About 1,400 people walked in procession, each with a blue ribbon around his neck.'

'They arrived at home in thirty-nine carriages, a little after ten at night. The females proceeded home, but the men, together with the bands, marched into the market place, where, after playing several enlivening airs, they concluded with "God Save the Queen" and three times three for Richard Cobden.'

The band received a mention in August 1846, when they performed at St Gregory's, Weldbank, near Chorley. The leader of the band was named as a Mr Butterfield.

Richard Cobden.

Also in 1846, on 3 October, the Crosse Hall Band appeared at Croston Wakes, where they played for the procession. 'The several bands were excellent, but the palm was given to the Crosse Hall Band, which headed the Druids and indeed, they played admirably, executing several waltzes and other pieces.'

A year later, on 23 January 1847, the paper refers to Mr Butterfield with his own band. 'Mr Butterfield's Quadrille Band played for a Tea Party and Ball at the King's Arms Inn, Chorley. The Ball was in connection with a select dancing class held by Mr Gorton.'

On 27 April 1850, the Crosse Hall Band 'appeared at the Assembly Room of the Royal Oak Inn, Chorley. The Concert consisted of overtures and other pieces by Mozart and Beethoven alongside a polka, waltz and a schottische. It was noted that the audience was from the "operative classes". After the Concert a Ball was held in the Assembly Room.' The article goes on to say, 'It is worthy of remark that the members of the Crosse Hall Band, who have made such proficiency in the performance of classical music, consist entirely of the working class. It is further proof, if such were needed, of how much may be accomplished by well-directed efforts.'

Again in 1850, on 5 October: 'Subscription Bowling Green: Wednesday last, being the close of the season, a Tea Party and Ball was held on the green and the weather being favourable for the purpose, the whole passed off in the most agreeable manner, to the evident satisfaction of all who took part in the proceedings. Some excellent matches were played, after which the company (which might consist of one hundred persons upward, included a goodly number of the fair sex) sat down to an excellent tea. Some of the most fashionable quadrilles were then danced upon the green by the company assembled, accompanied by a select portion of the Crosse Hall Band. A country dance, in which all joined, closed the entertainments on the green, when it was mutually agreed to adjourn to Mr Smith's large room at the Gillibrand Arms Inn, where the dancing was again resumed.'

The Crosse Hall Band appeared in 1851 and 1852 at the Alkaline Springs at Yarrow Bridge, Chorley described as 'a celebrated spa'. 24th May 1851: 'On Wednesday last, this favourite place of resort for pleasure parties was opened for the season. The Crosse Hall Band was in attendance and the amusements were kept up until a late hour.'

On 10 February 1852, the newspaper referred to the band as the Crosse Hall Quadrille Band, when they were engaged to play for a ball in the 'Catholic School Room in Euxton. During the evening they played for the most modern quadrilles.' On 28 February 1852 they played for 'a Tea Party and Ball at the George Inn, Chorley'.

It is interesting to note that the band was able to play for a procession during the day and then later play for a ball in the evening. Reported in June 1852: 'The Crosse Hall Band, headed the procession for the Friendly Societies in Mawdesley and then in the evening played for dancing at the Black Bull Inn, Mawdesley.'

The last time the band is mentioned is on 15 January 1853, when they attended a fund-raising event for a new schoolroom at Mount Pleasant Chorley. 'TEA PARTY AND BALL – The Crosse Hall Band was engaged for the occasion and played with their accustomed skill and spirit.'

String bands in Lancashire

WHAT'S in a name? Dance bands at the beginning of the nineteenth century were termed 'quadrille bands', reflecting the popularity of the new fashionable dances. This in turn became 'string band' in the second half of the century, before 'orchestral band' became popular. By the First World War this had become simply 'orchestra' or 'band'. in most cases the instrumentation in all these bands would remain similar.

Of course there were exceptions and as late as 12 February 1921, The *Lancaster Guardian* reported: 'An old fashioned Social was held in the Galgate

Institute on Tuesday, about 200 persons being present. Proceeds were for the Institute. Music was provided by the Galgate Quadrille Band.'

The first mention of the term 'string band' in Lancashire was in December 1857, when an advertisement appeared in connection with St Alban's Catholic church in Blackburn. 'St Alban's String Band appear under the leadership of George Ellis.'

In 1860, Gillett's String Band played at the Chorley Parish Church Bazaar. Some bands would play at concerts or provide background music to an event. In February 1871 there was a concert at Broughton known as the Broughton Penny Readings. These concerts included recitations, songs, readings and instrumental music. The Preston String Band played some tunes including 'Agnes Sorrel Quadrille' and 'The Light Bell Gallop'. Members of the band included Messrs J. Thornley and W. Norwood on violin.

The first time a Lancashire newspaper mentions a string band in the context of dancing is in November 1861, when Mr Gaulter's String Band played for a Tea Party and Ball in Darwen, for the local Power Loom Weavers' Association.

In 1876 Mr Warburton's String Band played for dancing at 'the Catholic Tea Party and Ball in Blackburn. The ball was held in the Exchange Hall and upwards of 1,400 persons sat down to tea.' In the same year the Padiham Amateur String Band were playing at the Assembly Room, Padiham. It lists the instrumentalists as '1st violin, Mr T. Wingham (leader); viola, Mr W. Wingham; vioilncello, Mr J. Pollard; D. Bass, Mr W. Livesey; cornet, Mr T. Moore; piano, Mr H. Helm.'

The Garstang Amateur String Band made an appearance in December 1878, when they provided the entertainment at the workhouse on Christmas Day. The article names the members of the band and their instruments: 'The members of the Garstang Amateur String Band acquitted themselves in most excellent style. Mr James Carr takes the lead with the concertina; Mr Thomas Carr, piccolo; Mr Ed. Till, first violin; Mr Jas. John Towers, second violin and Mr W. Till, violincello. The entertainment was a complete success.' The same band played in 1880 as part of an Old Folk's Concert in Garstang.

In December 1881 the Blackpool Amateur String Band played for a dance in the Queen's Hall, Fleetwood in aid of funds for the Fleetwood Cricket Club.

By the mid-1880s, towns and many small villages boasted their own string bands that would play for local events, but it wasn't until the end of the decade that it had become common practice for string bands to be playing for dances. By then it was commonplace for the organisers of balls and dances to be advertising the use of a string band as the term 'quadrille band' was gradually going out of favour.

There are very few references to female band leaders. This one is from 26 October 1901: 'The 17th Annual Catholic Ball took place on Wednesday night in the Public Hall, Leyland. The dancing took place to the strains of Miss Kayley's String Band.'

The term 'string band' continued up to and just after the First World War and the following account is a typical newspaper reference. 'On February 10th 1912 there was a Tea Party at St John's School, Whittle-le-Woods, for the Blackburn and District Branch of the Weavers, Winders and Warpers' Association. Dancing was to the strains of Marsden's String Band.'

However, as late as 13 March 1933, musicians were still described as being in a String Band. (See article about the Chipping String Band.)

Village band musicians (ink drawing), *Punch* magazine, 6 December 1911.

Matthew Wilson's Quadrille Band
(Lancaster)

MATTHEW WILSON was born in Dolphinholme in 1834. In the 1881 census, his address was given as 37 Penny Street, Lancaster, and his occupation was Barman (Inn). In fact, he also ran a musical instrument dealership from these premises at some juncture (see the advertisement below).

The first reference to Wilson's band is from the *Preston Chronicle* of 13 September 1873. 'GARSTANG FLORAL SHOW – There was music on both days. Mr Wilson's Quadrille Band from Lancaster was engaged, whose strains were a sore temptation to many, the pieces, without exception, being of a nature to incite to dance.'

The remaining references to the band are from the *Lancaster Guardian*. On 17 January 1874: 'The second Annual Tea Party and Ball in connection with the Furness and London and North Western Railway Companies' employees, took place on Friday last, at the Temperance Hotel, Carnforth, at which sixty couples attended. Dancing commenced about 8pm to the strains of an efficient Quadrille Band, under the leadership of Mr Wilson of Lancaster.'

QUADRILLE BAND.

M. WILSON'S old established Quadrille Band is OPEN TO RECEIVE ENGAGEMENTS, from two to five performers. Terms moderate
Address—M. WILSON, Musical Instrument Dealer, 37, Penny-street, Lancaster. [51-4

Lancaster Gazette, 15 December 1876.

On 7 July 1877: 'On Thursday week a picnic party from the neighbourhood of Burton-in-Lonsdale visited Hornby and Wray. The party, which was a very numerous one numbering 200, arrived in conveyances at about one o' clock and put up at the Castle Inn. The day being fine, tea was partaken in the open air, the table being spread in the field adjoining the inn. After the tea a dance took place on the greensward and then an adjournment was made to the large room adjoining the inn. Mr Wilson's Quadrille Band from Lancaster occupied the orchestra and dancing was kept up with spirit till twelve o' clock.'

On 26 October 1878: 'TENANTS' BALL AT QUERNMORE PARK – Wilson's Quadrille Band from Lancaster had been engaged for the occasion and to their strains dancing commenced shortly before eight o'clock, Mr Garnett leading off in the Triumph country dance with the wife of one of his Bleasdale tenants for a partner.'

On 3 January 1885: 'ODDFELLOWS' BALL – The Annual Ball promoted by the Lodges in Lancaster District of Oddfellows, the proceeds of which are now divided amongst the most necessitous widows in the district, was held in the Oddfellows' Hall. The orchestra was occupied by Mr M. Wilson's Quadrille Band, who played a popular selection of dance music.'

On 15 January 1887: 'On Thursday evening, the hall was the scene of another festive gathering, but on this occasion it was those of older growth who gathered together, namely the tenants and their families on the Thurnham and Bulk estates. Eight o'clock was the time fixed for assembling to participate in the Tenants' Ball and by that time 150 persons had congregated in the hall and whose ages ranged from those entering on the threshold of manhood or womanhood to those who were well advanced in years. Wilson's Band from Lancaster had been engaged.'

To celebrate Queen Victoria's Jubilee, the *Lancaster Guardian* reported on 25 June 1887 that 'Overton has not been behind the rest of the country in celebrating Her Majesty's Jubilee. A large marquee was erected in a field known as "Crooklands" kindly lent for the occasion by Mr T. Cottam. Mr Wilson's String Band from Lancaster was in attendance.'

A detailed list of the dances and music was given on 25 January 1890, when another account of the ball at Thurnham Hall was given. 'The Tenants' Ball took place at Thurnham Hall on Wednesday evening. About 200 of the tenants and their wives and in some cases sons and daughters attended. After all had supper, dancing was again resumed and went on until an early hour in the morning. The music was supplied by Mr Wilson's Band from Lancaster, the following being a list of the dances: Extra dance, "country dance"; 1 Quadrille, "The Rage of London"; 2 Waltz, "Love's Dreamland"; 3 Contra dance, "Haste to the Wedding"; 4 Lancers, "Mikado"; 5 Schottische, "Highland"; 6 Quadrille, "The Time"; 7 Polka, "Who's that Calling?"; 8 Contra dance "Going to the Market"; 9 Waltz, "Toreador"; 10 Lancers "Olivette"; 11 Gallop "Prestissimo"; 12 Quadrille "English Air"; 13. Polka, "Black and Tan"; 14 Contra dance, "The Triumph"; 15 Scottische, "The Fashionable"; 16 Lancers, "Lord of Lorne"; 17 Waltz, "Maid of the Mill"; 18 Quadrille, "Claribel"; 19 Gallop, "John Peel"; 20 Sir Roger de Coverley, "Addison".'

On 22 February 1890: 'WORKMEN'S SUPPER – To mark the near completion of the extensive repairs, alterations and change of the late barque "Perpetua" of Liverpool, to become "Annie Marshall" of Lancaster, the whole of the men in the employ of Messrs Nicholson and Marsh, Ship Yard, Glasson Dock, over fifty hands with their wives, to the number of little above 100, were provided with a first rate supper on Monday night at the Dalton Arms. The room was afterward cleared for dancing and to the strains of Mr Wilson's Band, it was vigorously kept up till twelve o'clock.' Also in 1890, on 6 December, there was a Tea Party and Ball in the Old Schoolroom, Galgate, for the Oddfellows. 'The tables were cleared and dancing commenced to the strains of Wilson's Quadrille Band. During the intervals, one of the members of the band played a few solos on the concertina.'

On 2 January 1892: 'READING ROOM BALL – One of the most successful and enjoyable balls ever held in Hornby took place on Wednesday evening at the Assembly Rooms, Castle Hotel, Hornby, in aid of the funds for the above Institute. An excellent selection of music was supplied by Wilson's Quadrille Band of Lancaster.'

On 24 September 1892: 'CONDER GREEN FLOWER SHOW. The thirty-fifth Annual Floral and Horticultural Show, held for the benefit of farmers and cottagers in the district south of Lancaster as far as Cockerham, was held at Conder Green on Wednesday. In the evening large numbers of people from Glasson, Thurnham and the surrounding district found their way to the little village for the purpose of either viewing the exhibits or dancing to the strains of Mr Wilson's Band, which played a selection of suitable music on the village green.'

Finally on 8 February 1893: 'On Friday evening, the 13th Annual Ball in connection with Lancaster and District Association of the National Union of Teachers, was held in the Phoenix Rooms and passed off with unequalled success. The company numbered 120 and the music was supplied by Mr Wilson's Orchestral Band.'

Robert Gudgeon's Band (Clitheroe)

AN obituary in the *Clitheroe Times* of 15 March 1895 gives an insight into the life and times of Robert Gudgeon. 'From his childhood, he was an assiduous musician, and though following the trade of shoemaking, was better known through his secondary and voluntary profession. He was born at Bunker's Hill, near Stonyhurst, in the December of 1843. His father was a shoemaker and, like his son who succeeded him, a clever musician. Mr Gudgeon senior was a somewhat successful violin maker and on one occasion won a Queen's Prize for the Best Specimen of Handiwork made by an Amateur, the winning article being a violin. It will be seen, then, that Mr Gudgeon came of a family in which musical taste was inherent to a remarkable degree. At a very early age his father made for him a fiddle with flat sides, and sometime after, an ordinary violin, in which his boyish spirit fairly revelled. He found great delight in his 'maturer' years in narrating the exploits of his childhood, when, with others of his companions, they would take their instruments and serenade the country people in the district.'

There are many references to his comic singing. The obituary continues, 'At one time Mr Gudgeon was considered the finest comic singer in Lancashire and Yorkshire. He took part in three first-class comic singing competitions and in all three was successful in carrying off first prize, one of the occasions being at the opening of Burnley Town Hall.'

Robert Gudgeon was well known in the Clitheroe area, both as a teacher of dancing and a bandleader. The *Clitheroe Times* went on to say that 'Mr Gudgeon possessed no little skill as a pianist and violinist and his services as a piano tuner were in great demand. Since he came to reside in the Borough, he never ceased to take the deepest interest in all musical affairs of the town. Mr Gudgeon leaves a widow, six sons and one daughter, most of whom have made headway in the musical world, some as vocalists and others as instrumentalists.'

The first time Robert Gudgeon is mentioned as leader of his own band was on 25 February 1882. 'On Tuesday evening, an Invitation Ball was held at the Lower Buck Hotel, Waddington, when there was a goodly number present. A special licence having been granted for the occasion, dancing was spiritedly engaged in until two o'clock to the strains of a band under the conductorship of Mr Gudgeon of Clitheroe.'

In March of the same year, the band was described as a Quadrille Band. 'St Patrick's Day was commemorated in Clitheroe with a Ball at the Swan and Royal Hotel, the house of Mr Lofthouse. A Quadrille Band, under the leadership of Mr Gudgeon, supplied the music.' There are references again in 1882, with balls at the Clitheroe Liberal Club, the Brownlow Arms Inn, Clitheroe, and again at the Lower Buck Hotel, Waddington.

On 30 January 1886, the band played at the Bicycle Club Ball. 'The Public Hall presented a very pretty spectacle on Friday evening, the occasion being the Annual Ball held under the auspices of the Clitheroe Bicycle Club. The orchestra was supplied by Mr Gudgeon's Band.'

The band regularly played at the Barrow Cricket Club Ball near Clitheroe. On February 25th 1888, the paper reports; 'On Saturday evening the Annual Ball in connection with the Barrow Cricket Club was held in a large room at the Whalley Abbey Printworks. The room was tastefully decorated and Mr Gudgeon's String Band very efficiently rendered the music.'

The band travelled as far as Blackburn. A report from 4 January 1890 informs its readership, 'BLACKBURN JUNIOR CONSERVATIVE CLUB BALL – The ball was held in the Town Hall Assembly Room on New Year's Eve. Mr Gudgeon's Band from Clitheroe occupied the orchestra.'

In Whalley, on 15 February 1893, the *Burnley News* reported, 'The Annual Assembly Ball in connection with Mr Gudgeon's dancing class took place on Friday in the Whalley Assembly Rooms and proved to be a great success, there being over 120 persons present. The room was elegantly decorated and the music was supplied by Mr Gudgeon's Band.'

Also, in March 1893, the band played for a fund-raising event. 'On Tuesday a ball in aid of the Bent Street Ragged School was held in the Exchange Assembly Rooms, Blackburn. Mr Gudgeon's Band occupied the orchestra and discoursed pleasant dance music.'

The last reference to the band is in the *Burnley Express* of 9 January 1895, just before Robert Gudgeon's death. 'The Annual Bicycle Club Ball was held last Thursday night in the Swan and Royal Hotel, Clitheroe. The ballroom was decorated for the occasion and presented a gay and most pleasing appearance. There were about 100 persons present and the music was supplied by Mr Gudgeon's Quadrille Band.'

Robert Gudgeon died on 9 March 1895 at his home in York Street, Clitheroe. The funeral took place at St Michael's and St John's Catholic Church in Clitheroe, where he had been a member of the choir.

BARROW CRICKET CLUB

THE

ANNUAL BALL

In connection with and for the benefit of the above named Cricket Club, will be held in the

Assembly Rooms, Whalley,

ON

FRIDAY, FEB. 16TH, 1894.

M.C's.:—A. M. HANSON, Esq., and L. MITCHELL, Esq.

Mr. GUDGEON'S BAND will play for Dancing.

Quadrilles at Eight oclock p.m.

REFRESHMENTS WILL BE PROVIDED.

TICKETS:— GENTLEMEN, 2s.; LADIES, 1s. 6d.

May be had from any member of the Committee and at the Door.

This advertisement is from a similar event and was the last known reference to Robert Gudgeon's Band. It was published a year before his death (1894).

With regard to Gudgeon's other musical interests, especially as a dance teacher, the following newspaper references suggest he was very popular and in much demand. From the *Blackburn Standard*, 15 April 1876: 'Mr Gudgeon's dancing class, which has been held in the Swan Hotel, Whalley, during the past winter months, closed with a Social Party on Friday last week, when 50 of his pupils and friends met together and enjoyed themselves in a pleasant manner until eleven o'clock.'

The *Preston Chronicle* of 3 February 1877 mentions 'Mr R. Gudgeon, the well-known humorous vocalist, who is equally as popular in several parts of Lancashire as a master of dancing, has been engaged for several months past in teaching that art to a number of ladies and gentlemen at the Starkie

Arms Hotel. A Quadrille Band, under the able leadership of Mr T.V. Carter, occupied the platform at one end of the room and discoursed a selection of music to the satisfaction of the company.'

One of Robert Gudgeon's dancing pupils was interviewed in 1960. He was Tom Holgate of Downham, near Clitheroe, who lived on a farm called Townley House. He came to live in the village in 1881 and had lived there ever since. Tom Holgate attended dancing classes at the Swan and Royal Hotel, Castle Street, when he was aged about sixteen (c.1889). These classes were run by Robert Gudgeon, with members of his family assisting him. The classes were for adults only and were held between 7 p.m. and 8 p.m. There was a period during the evening which was specifically allocated for tuition, with Mr Gudgeon demonstrating his steps whilst accompanying himself on the violin. 'Playing the violin, he waltzed across the floor with the proper step and we had to follow him.' After 8 p.m. they had a dance with little or no tuition. The classes were weekly and the charge was 2s. 6d. for a session of five or six weeks.

The Starkie Arms, Clitheroe.

At this point, Robert Gudgeon was aged about 50 or 60 years old. In the class he was assisted by one son, Ignatius, and a daughter, both of whom took various members of the class for dances. He also had a band, which was very much a family affair. He and one of his sons, James, both played the violin and another son played the 'big bass fiddle', whilst yet another played the piano and one of his remaining sons acted as reserve pianist. One 'outsider' played the flute for classes between 7 and 8 p.m. 'Sometimes old Mr Gudgeon played alone, but for general dancing he had his band.'

The dances which Tom Holgate learnt from Robert Gudgeon were 'Quadrilles, Lancers, Waltz Cotillion, Circassion Circle (couple meeting couple round the room), Roger de Coverley, Polka Mazurka, la Varsoviana, Waltz, Polka, Schottische and the Barn Dance.' He also learnt a Scottish reel, for which he was taught the 'steps' by Mr Gudgeon. He also learnt some from the school in Downham.

The classes at the Downham School were taken by William Blackburn, a man of between 20 and 30 years of age, who came from Clitheroe. He came to teach in the school once a week between 7 p.m. and 9 p.m. The classes were primarily for the children that had just left school, but did include some older children. Mr Blackburn provided the music for his

23

classes by playing the piano and the dances he taught were the same as those taught by Robert Gudgeon.[8]

William Blackburn was born in 1874 and was a musician. The Clitheroe Advertiser on 2 February 1897 reports, 'In connection with the Downham Cricket Club and Reading Room, a Social Gathering was held in the National School on Friday. Mr W.H. Blackburn accompanied the dancing.'

Robert Gudgeon's son John, who had been a member of his father's band, became a music teacher in Clitheroe and also had his own string band. On 28 January 1899 the Blackburn Standard reported, 'The 2nd Annual Ball of the Great Harwood Liberal Club took place last night. Mr John Gudgeon's Band played for dancing, which was kept up until three o'clock in the morning.'

John Gudgeon continued with the Cricket Club Ball. From the Blackburn Chronicle of 3 March 1900: 'Barrow Cricket Club held their Annual Ball at the Whalley Assembly Rooms. Mr J. Gudgeon's Band supplied the music.'

The remaining members of the Gudgeon family were also involved in playing for dances. On 13 October 1900, 'The opening of the New Town Hall at Great Harwood took place last night when a large number of the townspeople assembled at the Town Gate to witness the ceremony. Messrs Gudgeon's String Band was in attendance and played several selections.'

Members of Robert Gudgeon's Band are recalled in a book about life in Clitheroe. 'Robert Jackson, a music teacher in the town and leader of a flute and reed band, had been a member of three quadrille bands and played piccolo in each. The first was called Pollards Band and they practised at Mr Pollard's House, the New Inn. This band existed for eight years, after which he joined Matthew Duckett's String Band and played with them for many years. Robert Jackson's last musical involvement was with Robert Gudgeon's Band, his membership lasting for at least a dozen years.'[9]

Matthew Duckett had a band of some standing in the Clitheroe area. On 18 February 1882 the band played for a 'Workpeople's Dinner' at the Swan and Royal Hotel in Clitheroe. This was for the 'Winders and Warpers' employed at Mercer and Hodgson's Holme Mill. 'Dancing was engaged in to the strains of Mr Matthew Duckett's Quadrille Band, the intervals between the dances being occupied in the singing of songs by various members of the company.'

J.W. Collinson's String Band (Preston)

JOHN WILLIAM COLLINSON was born in 1856 in Preston. His father, Samuel, had been a 'professor of music' and had his own quadrille band. Living at Elizabeth Street, Preston and while only fifteen years of age, John himself was already being regarded as a 'professor of music'. An article in the *Liverpool Mercury* of 15 April 1895 outlined his life and career to date: 'Mr J.W. Collinson, the new musical director at the Blackpool Victoria Pier was born in Preston and was the son of a most excellent musician and teacher. The family moved to London when he was quite young but he returned to Lancashire and lived for a time in Liverpool, where he became leader of the Alexandra Theatre Orchestra.'

His band followed in the footsteps of the previous Lancashire Quadrille Bands like Horabins, Haslams and Norwoods. They would play at the most prestigious events in the towns and cities within the region and in the

Mr J.W. Collinson's String Band [10]

largest halls and assembly rooms. The band was involved in the celebrations for the opening of the Preston Docks in 1892.

The boy in the photograph is Arthur Catterall, described as 'the wonder boy violinist from Lancashire'. He later became leader of the Halle Orchestra in Manchester.

The photograph of the eight members of the band, plus Arthur Catterall, was taken in the prestigious Harris Museum and Art Gallery, Preston. All the band members are dressed in a military style uniform, but the gentleman with the violin, seated second from the left, is wearing a compatible jacket, but of a different style. This could well single him out as being the leader, John William Collinson.

His band played throughout the north-west of England and North Wales, although he continued to play at functions in his home town of Preston. Although the band mainly played for concerts, they did play for dancing and on 7 December 1889, 'The members of the Harris Choir had, on the evening of Monday last, a delightful reunion, when they were invited to a Soiree and Ball. The Preston Public Hall was prettily decorated for the occasion. Mr J.W. Collinson performed some pieces on his violin. At 10 o' clock the Ball started, the music being provided by Mr. J. W. Collinson and his Band.'

On 2 March 1889: 'The Annual Invitation Ball under the auspices of our local Artillery Volunteer Sergeants came off Wednesday night in the Preston Public Hall. A very efficient band under the direction of Mr. Collinson occupied the orchestra. The dance programme included 22 well varied dances, which concluded in the early hours of the next morning. Miss Richardson of Fishergate supplied a very excellent supper and a goodly number partook of it. The bars were the charge of Mr. Whiteside of the Peel Hall Inn and Mr. Miller of the New Inn.'

The Official Opening of Preston Docks was carried out on Saturday 25 June 1892 by Prince Albert, Duke of Edinburgh, and the second son of Queen Victoria. He arrived in Preston the previous day and travelled to 'Darwen Bank', the Mayor of Preston's residence in Walton-le-Dale. The account in the *Preston Chronicle* of 25 June 1892 describes the procession from Preston Railway Station. 'After the Royal party had passed School Lane last night a procession was formed from St Aidan's Schoolyard. The Bamber Bridge Brass Band and the Higher Walton Band preceded the Bamber Bridge Morris Dancers.' At the Mayor's residence, 'During the dinner, Mr. Collinson's String Band played a choice selection of music.'

Preston Guardian, 10 December 1881.

VIOLIN.—Mr. J. W. COLLINSON, of Liverpool, will visit Preston weekly to receive Pupil.—For terms, &c. apply, Mr. T. THORPE, Choral Society's Offices, Lune-street.

MR. COLLINSON'S LONG NIGHT on NEW YEAR'S EVE. Gentlemen, 1s 6d; Ladies, 1s.—4, St. James's-road, Moor Park.

Preston Guardian, 26 December 1891.

On 16 March 1893 the *Liverpool Mercury* reported that 'Last evening the Mayor of Bootle gave an "At home" at Bootle Town Hall, which was attended by 600 ladies and gentlemen. Mr J.W. Collinson's Band provided the music and dancing continued on until twelve o'clock.'

Finally, on 2 May 1900, again in The *Liverpool Mercury*: 'Last evening the Lord Mayor and Lady Mayoress gave the 2nd of their Receptions to the Nurses of the Hospitals and Charitable Institutions of the city. The music for the dancing was provided by Collinson's Orchestra.'

John William Collinson's official residence on 12 January 1908 was 24 Carton Avenue, Sefton Park, Liverpool. He died that year, aged 52.

Bateson's Band
(Furness and South Lakes)

THE first steamboat to operate on an English lake was the *Lady of the Lake*, built in 1845 and launched with a ceremony at Newby Bridge at the southern tip of Lake Windermere. She was built by Richard Ashburner of Greenodd for the Windermere Steam Yacht Company. The *Westmorland Gazette* reported on 26 July 1845 that 'The Band of the Kendal Cavalry entertained passengers on the maiden voyage to Ambleside and dancing took place on the top deck.'

The Furness Railway Company owned a number of steamers on Windermere and often employed bands to provide music for the passengers. The boats travelled the length of Windermere, from Lakeside at the southern end to Waterhead (Ambleside) at the top of the lake, stopping at Bowness on the eastern side.

The photograph below of Bateson's Band aboard the *Swan* is the earliest known image of the band. It came from a collection of photographs of the Bowness area, which had the following information attached: 'Here is a typical orchestra on the Swan. The bands were a popular feature on boats, playing to the visitors. A number of bands existed from time to time, the Bijou Band and Bateson's Band being perhaps the best known.'[11]

There is a reference to the Bijou Band in the *Westmorland Gazette* on 31 January 1903. 'The Annual Ball in connection with the Bowness Conservative Club was held in the Windermere Institute on Thursday evening. The music was supplied by the Bijou Band.'

Bateson's Band had performed for the Furness Railway Company since

Bateson's Band on board the steamer
Swan, Lake Windermere *c*.1896.

1859 and it had been established by John E. Bateson, born in Wortley, Leeds, in 1822. The 1881 census shows the family living at Undermillbeck, Bowness, and he was listed as a musician/labourer.

Many of the musicians in the band had other jobs. For example, George Rhodes of Woodside Cottages, Bowness-on-Windermere, pictured on board the Swan holding a flute, was a plasterer by trade. He was born in 1865 and also originally came from Leeds.

The Era, 18 June 1887.

WANTED, to Join not later than Monday, Good Second Cornet, for Windermere Steam Yachts Band. Terms, shares. No opposition. J. BATESON, Waterloo Fair, Bowness, Windermere.

There must have been a need to augment the band during the busy tourist season on Lake Windermere. Advertisements were placed in the *The Era* national newspaper looking for a range of instrumentalists. The one below has a contact address in Bowness with John Bateson as the contact.

John's son, Thomas E. Bateson, born at Bowness in 1863, was also described as a musician/labourer. He played the cornet and can be seen

28

fourth from the left in the photograph. He succeeded his father as leader of the band and they continued to play until 1914, when the First World War intervened. The next advertisement shows Thomas as the leader of the Windermere Steam Yacht Band.

Besides working on the boats, the band also played at dances and galas in the area. There are accounts of the band playing for dances on the green in front of the Old England Hotel at Bowness and across the lake at the Ferry Hotel, Sawrey, which at the time of the article was in Lancashire. The hotels had become favourite destinations for the many tourists who were attracted to the Lake District in Victorian times. Playing on the boats for tourists was seasonal and so the band would play for dances in the district during the evenings and particularly in the winter.

The *Westmorland Gazette* of 23 July 1898 reported that 'the children attending Bowness St Mary's School had their Annual Treat. Here the usual forms of amusements were indulged in, additional brightness being given to the proceedings by the playing of the Steam Yacht Band.'

WANTED, Engagement by Solo and Second Cornets, Tenor, Euphonium, and Bombardon, together or separate. T. BATESON, Leader, W. S. Y. Band, Bowness, Windermere.

Saturday, 6 October 1888.

Bateson's Windermere Steam Yacht and Lakeside Pavilion Orchestra

BATESON'S WINDERMERE STEAM YACHTS and LAKESIDE PAVILION ORCHESTRA.

This postcard is the band's official studio photograph for the Furness Railway Company and indicates that the band had a dual role, both playing at the Lakeside Pavilion and on board the steam yachts. Thomas Bateson can be seen on the back row holding the cornet. The fiddle player on the front row is Thomas's wife Maud, born in Ireland in 1879.

MUSICIANS WANTED.

WANTED, for the Windermere Lake
Steamers, to open June 1st, First Violin as Leader,
with Music; Second Violin, Piccolo, 'Cello, Bass, Trombone.
Terms, shares. No opposition. T BATESON, Bowness, Windermere.

WINDERMERE STEAM YACHT BAND.

WANTED, To Open, Monday, July 23d,
Competent Harpist, Clarionet, and Flautist. Must be
Steady and Attentive to Business. State Age, Sa'ary, or
Shares. Apply, BATESON, the Bothy, Bowness and Winder-
mere

LEFT *The Era* newspaper, 15 May 1897.

RIGHT *The Era*, 21 July 1900.

Perhaps Thomas Bateson took charge of more than one orchestra as the following advertisements show. The first of June would tie in with the start of the season and there were a number of steamers on Windermere. *The Era* contained pages of advertisements either recruiting particular musicians or where a musician or band would be offering their services. It is surprising the number of harpists that were available.

Passengers would be able to hear the band as they arrived or waited in the Pavilion building. The station lies at the southern end of Windermere and the terminus of the Lakeside to Haverthwaite branch of the Furness Railway. The photograph below shows six members of the band, sitting behind music stands. In all photographs of the band, the harpist is always to the right side of the band and the double bass player to the left.

Bateson's Orchestral Band on the balcony of the Pavilion.[12]

The Furness Railway Company's
Ferry Band, *c*.1910.

Furness Ferry Band

THE Furness Railway Company introduced a ferry service across Morecambe Bay between Barrow-in-Furness and Fleetwood in 1900. An advertisement for the service shows that it provided a link between Blackpool and the Lake District, with a connecting tram service from Fleetwood into Blackpool. From Barrow, passengers could take the scheduled Furness Railway services to Coniston or Lakeside, Windermere.

The ferry crossings continued until 1914 and the outbreak of the First World War. Four paddle steamers, including *Lady Margaret* and *Lady Evelyn*, were operated but, sadly, the steamers did not resume their service once the war was over.

The instruments in the above photograph are very similar to those utilised in Bateson's Band, who were also employed by the Furness Railway Company. The one noticeable difference is the absence of a double bass; the harp seems to have been an acceptable instrument in this kind of small string band.

As with Bateson's Steam Yacht Band on Windermere, the railway company also employed musicians to provide entertainment for passengers on board the ferries as well as at the terminals.

The ferry sailings were seasonal, operating from Whitsuntide until the end of September. It is unclear whether the Furness Ferry Band continued to function as a dance band for the remainder of the year and where they were based also remains a mystery. It would either have been Fleetwood or Barrow-in-Furness, with the latter being most probable.

John Thorne's String Band (Adlington)

JOHN THORNE was involved in local village life as the following newspaper extracts illustrate. The first reference to his band is in the *Chorley Guardian* of 13 January 1881. 'An Invitation Ball was held in the Co-operative Hall, Adlington, on New Year's Eve. Dancing commenced at 9 o'clock, to the strains of Mr John Thorne's String Band.'

John Thorne was born in Adlington in 1854. He initially worked in a local cotton mill, but by 1888 he had become a teacher of stringed instruments as the following advertisement shows.

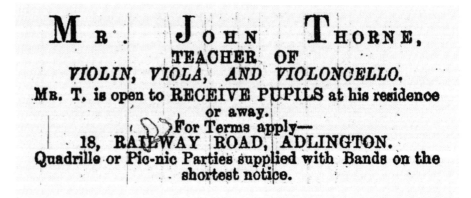

Chorley Standard, 21 July 1888.

From the *Chorley Guardian* of 11 October 1890: 'A number of people of the Ellerbeck Colliery Company assembled at the White Bear Hotel, Adlington, on Saturday last. Mr Thorne officiated as the violinist – songs were given by Messrs W. McDonald, J. Baxter, A. Band, G. Holme, J.E. Turner, T. Prescott and W. Cornwall, there was also a clog dance by J.E. Turner. Mr Thorne gave a violin solo, The Bluebells of Scotland.'

The same newspaper, on 5 December 1896, reports 'On Saturday last, the directors of the Birkacre Co. Ltd, entertained their workpeople and tenants to a Tea Party and Dance in honour of the marriage of Mr J.W. Thom. Tea was served at 4 o'clock and afterwards dancing continued until 11 o'clock. Mr Thorne's excellent String Band provided the music.'

On 7 January 1899, the *Chorley Guardian* provided details of the members of the band. 'ADLINGTON WORKPEOPLE'S PARTY – On Saturday last the workpeople at Springfield Mill were entertained to a Sandwich Tea. Excellent music for dancing was supplied by Mr J. McCarthy (violin), Mr S. Leeming (violin), Mr T. Lee (violin), Mr J. Thorne (bass) and Mr D. Thorne (clarinet).'

'Mr Thomas C. Catterall of Leicester Mill Quarries', reported the *Chorley Standard* on 1 February 1902, 'gave an excellent dinner for his employees and wives at the Elephant and Castle Hotel, Adlington. Mr Thorne's Band occupied the orchestra and played a good selection of dance music.'

The last reference to John Thorne's Band was on 2 January 1915, when the *Chorley Guardian* told of an event organised by the local Conservative Party. 'As usual there was a large attendance at the 17th Annual Ball arranged by the Adlington Conservatives. Excellent dance music was provided by Mr Thorne's String Band.'

Edward Knowles' String Band (Leyland)

EDWARD HILTON KNOWLES, who was born in 1871, lived at 'Listz House' in Sandy Lane, Leyland. By the age of 18, he was a pianist and leader of the Leyland String Band in their first newspaper reference in 1889. He was also organist and choirmaster at Leyland parish church.

By 1892 he was the leader his own band, the Edward Knowles String Band. A newspaper report of January 13th 1892 reveals that 'On Wednesday evening, the 10th Annual Charity Tea Party and Ball took place at the Railway Hotel. The proceedings commenced with an excellent knife and fork tea, to which about 300 people sat down. The floor of the ballroom was rendered the more appreciable by its having been thoroughly waxed for the occasion. The room was tastefully decorated, the widows being draped with lace curtains, while quantities of ferns were used in the decoration of the interior. Dancing commenced about seven o'clock to the capital strains of Mr E. H. Knowles' String Band.'

Three days later: 'The 1st Annual Tradesmen's Ball was held in the Infants' National Schoolroom, Union Street, on Wednesday evening and was in every respect a great success. An efficient band under the conductorship of Mr. Knowles discoursed admirable dance music.'

The National School Rooms became a favourite venue for dances in

Leyland. On 2 September 1893: 'On Saturday evening, a Ball, promoted by the Leyland Cricket Club, took place in the National Schoolroom, Union Street. Mr Kirkman, gardener at Broadfield, decorated the school. Mr Knowles' String Band provided the music for dancing'. There was a similar ball on 3 October, at the same venue, for the Leyland Cycling Club.

On 23 December 1894: 'The Leyland Morris Dancers held their Annual Ball at the National School, Union Street, on Thursday evening and the affair passed off most successfully. There was a good attendance. The music was supplied by Mr Knowles' String Band. Messrs Whalley and Bentley made excellent MCs.'

On 8 February 1896: On Wednesday evening, the 14th Annual Tea Party and Ball in aid of St Mary's Mission, took place in the Railway Hotel, Leyland. Dancing commenced to the strains of Mr Knowles' String Band and continued until three o'clock in the morning.'

In the same venue, reported on 20 February 1897: 'The Annual Leyland Catholic Tea Party and Ball took place at the Railway Hotel Assembly Rooms. Mr E.H. Knowles' Quadrille Band provided the music.'

Edward Knowles' band again provided the music for the Leyland Morris Dancers on 16 December 1899. 'The Morris Dancers held their Annual Ball on Thursday evening in the New Public Hall, when the guests numbered about 100 and a very pleasing picture was presented by the Morris Dancers in their picturesque costume. The ladies were mostly attired in evening dress. The music was provided by Mr Knowles' Band.'

Finally on 3 March 1900: 'A well-attended Ball, promoted by the Leyland Choral Society, took place on Friday week. A capital programme of dance music was supplied by Mr E.H. Knowles' String Band.'

The *Chorley Standard* published an article on 28 March 1903, which announced the death of Edward Knowles. He was only 32 years of age when he died; his widow Margaret was 31. The Leyland parish magazine of April 1903 printed an article about his funeral, commenting that he was greatly respected in Leyland and that the church had been full for the service.

Higher Walton String Band

HIGHER WALTON is a small mill village situated between Preston and Blackburn. It was dominated by a large cotton spinning mill owned by the Rodgett family who lived in a large house in nearby Walton-le-Dale known as Darwen Bank.

Despite its size, Higher Walton fielded three musical bands, namely Higher Walton Brass Band, Higher Walton String Band and Higher Walton Handbell Ringers.

The Brass Band performed at a gala in the village on 2 July 1888. 'This afternoon, the Sports and Gala promoted by the Higher Walton Football Club came off on the football ground before a fair attendance of spectators. The Higher Walton Brass Band played at intervals during the afternoon for dancing.'

The Brass Band has already been mentioned in the article about John W. Collinson, when they played for the Bamber Bridge Morris Dancers in a procession to Darwen Bank as part of the opening of the Preston Docks celebrations in 1892.

The first reference to The Higher Walton String Band was on 29 October 1892, when they played in the nearby village of Walton-le-Dale. 'A public meeting in connection with the above was held on Wednesday evening, in the Wesleyan Schoolroom. The Higher Walton String Band, under the conductorship of Mr C.F. Jackson, gave several selections of music.'

In the *Blackburn Standard* on 14 January 1893: 'On Wednesday evening, the Higher Walton Band of Hope Society held a meeting in the Wesleyan School. Selections of music were given by the Higher Walton String Band.'

On 3 February 1894, the *Preston Guardian* reported that the band had organised a concert in Higher Walton village. 'The proceeds from the concert are for the purpose of defraying the debt on the String Band piano.'

These three articles only mention the string band playing in a concert setting. However, an advertisement does show that they were available for other functions and could be booked for a function at the address of the conductor.

THE HIGHER WALTON STRING BAND is open to receive Engagements for Concerts, Bazaars, Garden Parties, &c.—For terms apply to Mr. C. F. Jackson, 3, Woodland View, Walton-le-Dale.

5 September 1903.

On the same date there is an article about the band appearing at a temperance meeting in the Wesley Schoolrooms in Higher Walton. The guest speaker was the Rev. A. Crouhart, vicar of the nearby All Saints' Church.

The photograph of the Higher Walton String Band was taken outside All Saint's Vicarage, Higher Walton, around 1910. In the centre of the front

The Higher Walton String
Band, *c.*1910.[13]

row is Alice Ferrier, wife of the headmaster, William Ferrier (sitting to
her left), of All Saints' School in Higher Walton. William and Alice Ferrier
were the parents of Kathleen Ferrier, the world famous contralto singer,
who was born in 1912. William Ferrier was the pianist in the string band
and was born in Aintree, near Liverpool, in 1878.

In the first chapter of a book about Kathleen Ferrier, her sister Winifred
refers to her father's interest in music. The article mentions that 'he was
an amateur pianist and joined forces with a fiddler and flautist to form a
small band, playing for many local dances.'[14]

Members of the Higher Walton Handbell Ringers
also played with the string band. Henry Brierley
was the conductor of the handbell ringers and was
described as 'a sidesman in the church and also a
member of the fiddle group in the village.' William
King, sitting to the extreme right of the front row
in the photograph, was also identified as one of the handbell ringers.[15]

THE HIGHER WALTON HANDBELL RINGERS
are Open for Engagements, for Concerts, Parties, &c.
Terms moderate.—O. Clarke, 22, Church-terrace, Higher
Walton.

10 January 1903.

James Winder's Band (Wyresdale)

NEWSPAPER references of James Winder's Band are rare; this one
is from the *Lancaster Guardian* of 4 January 4th. 'ABBEYSTEAD
BALL – The annual function was held in the Schoolroom on New Year's

Eve, when there was a large attendance; over forty couples being present. The music was provided by James Winder's Band.'

A member of the Winder family is mentioned in a report in the *Lancaster Guardian* of 16 February 1889. 'On Monday evening, the little hamlet of Abbeystead presented an unusual appearance of gaiety, the reason being the Ball held in the Schoolroom, about 100 ladies and gentlemen being present. The company began to assemble about seven o'clock and dancing interspersed with songs was pursued with unflagging delight and spirit until nine. (After supper) dancing was again resumed with the same spirit until three o'clock in the morning. Among those who favoured the company with songs were Messrs Remmington, Parker, Armer and Smith. Messrs Parker, Melrose Rimmington and Winder supplied the music.'

James Winder's grandson, Bill Winder, still lives in Dolphinholme. He is custodian of two surviving manuscript books from the earlier days of the Winder family's involvement with dance music and he is also very knowledgeable about six of the musicians depicted in the above photograph.

James Winder (1874–1954) is seated centre of the three fiddle players in the middle row. He was the leader of the band, which included three of his brothers. At the front, with fiddle, is his brother Edward Winder

James Winder's Band, *c.*1910.

37

(1872–1949). To James's right, also with fiddle, is John Winder, and behind James with a cornet is Thomas Winder. The man with the harp is William Brockbank. Sitting next to him with the fiddle is Ted Pearson. Bill did not know the names of the others, but he knew that Thomas Winder and some of the other members of the band did not return from the First World War.

The Winder family were dairy farmers who lived in the hamlet of Greenbank in Wyresdale, near the village of Dolphinholme. What makes the Winder family so fascinating is their musical heritage, which goes back many generations, certainly to the latter half of the eighteenth century. They played music for dancing and taught dancing in their native north Lancashire, where the members of the family who actually did the teaching were customarily referred to as Dancing Masters.

The band played at all the local dances around Wyresdale and at hiring fairs in the Trough of Bowland and as far as Slaidburn. At these fairs, farmers would negotiate with potential employees to determine their following year's wages. The band would set out the day before, travelling by horse and trap. They would play from eight o'clock on the evening of the fair until about two o'clock in the morning. There were times when extra money or a gallon of ale from the local pub would persuade the musicians to continue playing for far longer.

Bill Winder was not sure how much of the music contained in the manuscript books, handed down through the generations would still be being played by the band in the photograph. He did know, however, that the band continued playing after the First World War and on into the 1930s. They also introduced a few new dances and tunes into their repertoire to reflect the new fashions, which would suggest they probably had a constantly evolving repertoire.[16]

Bill Winder possesses two handwritten manuscript books from the Winder family, dating back to the early nineteenth century. His cousin David Pearcy, has a book dated 1789 and inscribed 'John Winder, Dancing Master'. These books include a collection of dance tunes; some are well known and some are unique with titles referring to places in the local area, including Pilling Moss, Tarnbrook Rant and Chipping Fair.[17]

May Pearcy from Over Wyresdale, provided the photograph of the band in which her father and two uncles appear. She remembered that her grandfather, James Winder, played the cello for the church services at Over Wyresdale Church, before the organ was introduced. There remains a collection of instruments in the church, consisting of flutes, clarinets and a cello.

From the 1890s onwards, dances took place in the village school, the village hall and the old warehouse in Dolphinholme Mill. At sheep shearing time, farmers would often provide a meal for the workers and either a local fiddler or a band would then play for dancing.

Children learned the dances in classes, which usually took place in the granaries on a number of farms in Over Wyresdale. 'They had a chap to play the concertina' and all the children of the neighbourhood gathered there. The classes were informal and the older children taught the younger ones. Dancing took place at weddings and parties in the farmhouses throughout Wyresdale. The supper was held in the house and dancing took place in the hayloft, over the top of the cows! Sometimes they would have to take turns in going to the house for the food.

May Pearcy started going to dances in Wyresdale shortly before the First World War, the programme usually starting with a Waltz, followed by a Barn Dance, and a set of the Lancers. Other popular dances were the Quadrilles, Waltz-Cottillon, Polka, Varsoviana, Schottische, Military 2 Step, Veleta, Highland Schottische, Cottagers, and on occasions, they would end the night with Sir Roger De Coverley.

Cecil Sharp, the acclaimed dance and song collector, visited Dophinholme in 1911. He collected material from the Winder family, including the music and dance notation for the 'Three man Greensleeves dance'. Two of the three dancers who performed for Cecil Sharp on that occasion were James and John Winder.[18]

William Brockbank and other local musicians

T HE harpist, William Brockbank, was born in the village of Scorton, north of Garstang in 1857. He later moved to Dolphinholme Bottom, where he lived with his wife Annie and their five children. Bill Winder recalled that he was a popular character and would sometimes walk to dance venues with his harp strapped to his back. He was affectionately referred to by the locals as 'Old Brockie'. He lived to the age of 79 and died in Lancaster on 28 July 1936. He is buried in the churchyard at St Mark's in the village of Dolphinholme.

There are many detailed references to William Brockbank in local newspapers, primarily the *Lancaster Guardian*. He was closely linked to other

William Brockbank.

musicians and bands in Galgate and Wyresdale, some of whom feature in the references below.

The first article about William appeared on 25 March 1882. 'ELLEL COTTAGE LODGE; FRIENDLY ORDER OF MECHANICS — The Anniversary of the above Lodge was celebrated on Saturday last, at the Green Dragon Hotel, Galgate, by a Dinner and Ball. 142 members and friends partook of the dinner, which was served in excellent style by the host, Mr James Jackson. Dancing was afterwards spiritedly indulged in to the strains of the harp and dulcimer, presided over by Messrs Brockbank and Gabbat of Dolphinholme.' William Gabbat, the dulcimer player, was born in Wyresdale in 1859.

The use of a dulcimer for dancing, it seems, was not unusual. In nearby Wray, in the Lune Valley, there was an event in the village schoolroom on 10 February 1883, when 'Dancing was resumed after supper to the strains of Mr B. Clarkson's dulcimer'.

Yet another dulcimer is mentioned on 31 January 1888, at a social for the Galgate Branch of the Lancaster and Skerton Co-operative Society. 'On Tuesday night there was a Tea Party and Ball, when about 200 partook of tea, after which dancing was indulged in to the strains of Messrs Downham (piccolo) and Fearing (dulcimer).' These two musicians were also members of the local Brass Band. Stephen Thomas Downham, born in Quernmore, near Lancaster, in 1868, was a cornet player in Galgate Brass Band and James Fearing, born in Galgate in 1865, was its Bandleader.[19]

Just two musicians are mentioned in an item published on 9 March 1889. 'The members of the Friendly United Order of Mechanics held their Tea Party and Ball in the large Schoolroom. After tea the room was cleared for dancing and Messrs Brockbank and Gabbat of Dolphinholme were the instrumentalists. At intervals during the evening songs were rendered by Messrs J. Wright, Jas. Johnson and J. Walmsley.'

On 28 September 1889: 'The Galgate Gaslight Flower Show took place in the old Schoolroom. The flowers were staged in the lower room, the upper room being devoted to dancing, which was kept up to between eleven and twelve each evening to the music of Downham's Quadrille Band.'

As well as the harp, William Brockbank played the piano. A report in the *Lancaster Gazette*r of 27 December 1890 reveals that William Brockbank played in a concert at Dolphinholme School. He formed part of the evening's entertainment when 'Mr Brockbank played the piano to accompany Mr and Miss Tysoe (violins).' At Galgate on 21 March 21st, he was also playing for dancing, this time at the Co-operative Tea Party in the large schoolroom. 'Dancing was afterwards freely indulged in, and kept up till about one o'clock the next morning, to the strains of Messrs Downham, Fearing and Brockbank's Quadrille Band.'

The following *Lancaster Guardian* report refers to the annual Ellel Horticultural Show, held in September 1891. 'During the afternoon Downham's Quadrille Band was present and played a selection of music. At six o'clock the room was cleared for dancing, which was kept up till midnight, the music being supplied by the above band.'

There seems to be ample evidence to indicate that local musicians would regularly join in loose associations to form impromptu bands, which would consist of whatever instrumentation the players happened to bring. Reporting on 15 January 1898, the same newspaper states that 'An Invitation Ball took place in the large Schoolroom, Galgate, on Friday. Dancing commenced at 8 p.m. and continued until three in the morning. The band consisted of Messrs Wright (piano), Downham (flute) and Brookes (cornet).'

The following three references are taken from the *Preston Guardian*. Firstly, on 11 February 1899, the paper reports on the Dolphinholme Reading Room Committee having organised a celebration. 'DOLPHINHOLME READING ROOM – To celebrate the return of the library, the members arranged a dance for Thursday evening. The music was supplied by Mr Brockbank.'

The following year, in the 13 January (1900) edition, readers were informed of a 'DANCE AT DOLPHINHOLME – A successful dance organised by the Reading Room Committee was held in the Library in Dolphinholme one last night week. There were present between sixty and seventy persons who thoroughly enjoyed themselves. Mr Brockbank supplied the music.'

A fifteen-mile journey at a potentially difficult time of the year faced William Brockbank in January 1903. 'On Friday the Annual Young Peoples' Ball was held in the Wray Assembly Room and proved again to be a very successful event. Dancing was kept up until 2 a.m. to the strains of Brockbank's Band (Dolphinholme).'

A week later, on 31 January, he is booked to play again, but this time nearer home. 'The Annual Tea Party, Concert and Dance in connection with St Mark's Church took place on Tuesday in the Reading Room, Dolphinholme. Mr Brockbank's Band discoursed the music for dancing.'

A report on 30 January 1904: 'DOLPHINHOLME VILLAGE READING ROOM; LONG NIGHT DANCE – This annual function, which is looked forward to with great interest, was held in the Reading Room on Thursday last week. The night was all that could be desired, no small matter for the success of a country dance. The room when lit up and when the dance was at its "gayest", made a very attractive picture. The music was supplied by Mr Brockbank's Village Band.'

The 'Long Night' refers to an evening of song, dance and recitations. Special events of this nature would quite often last through the night. 'Mr Brockbank's Village Band' suggests that its membership might well have been made up of musicians all local to Dolphinholme village. If that were so, it is almost certain that some members of the Winder family would have been included in their number, adding veracity to the words 'the night was all that could be desired.'

William Brockbank is mentioned again in November 1904. 'The first of a series of dances, promoted by the Dolphinholme Reading Room Committee, took place on Thursday evening week. The affair was a great success, there being a large number present. Dancing took place to the music of Mr Brockbank's Band.'

On 9 January 1909: 'A social was held in the large Schoolroom, Galgate, on New Year's Eve. Music for dancing was supplied by Messrs Fearing and Brockbank.'

On 5 February 1910: 'ELLEL COTTAGE LODGE OF MECHANICS – The Annual Tea Party and Ball took place in the large School, Galgate, on Saturday, when over 180 members and friends partook of tea. Dancing took place in the upper room, the music being supplied by Messrs Curwen, Fearing and Brockbank.' For the same event on February 18th 1911, the band consisted of Downham, Curwen and Wilkinson.

The first time a member of the Winder family was mentioned together with William Brockbank was on 17 February 1912, even though the photograph above, taken around 1910, shows William Brockbank as a member of James Winder's Band. 'The Annual Tea Party and Ball of the Ellel Lodge, was held in the large Schoolroom, Galgate, on Saturday. About 200 partook in an excellent tea and then dancing took place in the upper rooms. Messrs Brockbank, Fearing and Winder provided the music for dancing.'

There is an account of dancing in Galgate on 21 February 1920. 'A Social and Dance was held on Tuesday evening in the Galgate Institute; there were about 130 present. Old fashioned dances were indulged including the 'three reel', which amused the younger generation.'

Finally on 12 February 1921: 'An old fashioned Social was held in the Institute on Tuesday, about 200 persons being present. Proceeds were for the Institute. Music was provided by the Galgate Quadrille Band.'

Blackpool Central Pier Orchestra

D URING the annual Wakes weeks, the designated holiday periods when the mills and industry would traditionally shut down for two weeks, many people from across the north of England would pack their cases and catch the train to Blackpool. Among the many attractions at this famous resort would be the opportunity to dance on the Central Pier.

The *Preston Guardian* reported on 7 August 1880: 'BANK HOLIDAY – Beautiful weather favoured the excursionists who journeyed down to Blackpool on Monday. The North Pier was exceedingly well patronised throughout the day. On the South Pier, a band was continually playing for dancing which was well kept up.'

The building of Blackpool's second pier was motivated by the immense popularity of the North Pier among the upper classes. South Pier, as it was

Open air dancing on Blackpool's Central Pier (originally South Pier), 1897.

initially called, catered for the opposite end of the market. As the Director of North Pier said at the time, 'I think it is a good idea that the working classes can enjoy themselves without the surveillance of the other classes'. Despite complaints from the residents of central Blackpool (dancing was perceived to lower the tone of an area), building of the new pier was started in June 1867 and completed in May 1868, in time for the summer season. South Pier was the most popular place in the whole of Blackpool for open-air dancing with Quadrille bands playing polkas, barn dances, lancers and quadrilles from as early as 5.30 a.m. until late into the night. In 1873 the bands were being paid £3 10s. weekly (Sundays extra) and in 1886 a nine piece band was hired for a fixed rate of £12 7s. 6d. a week.[20]

The commercial success of the two piers in Blackpool prompted a smaller third pier to be built a little further to the south. This additional pier was opened in 1893 and at first was known as the Victoria Pier. The intention was to cater for more upmarket tastes, but in reality its market gradually levelled out catering for family recreation. Through common association, the three piers gradually became known as the North Pier, Central Pier (being the original South Pier) and the later South Pier (which had started life as Victoria Pier).

In a debate about an extension to the Central Pier and the possible problems with the dancers near the entrance, the *Preston Guardian* reported on 13 June 1891: 'Last Whit Monday 20,000 persons used the pier. Questions were then asked of witnesses and two police inspectors as to the dancing that went on at the pier. Each said that the Lancashire people who visited the town were very fond of dancing and one witness said that it was carried out from six in the morning until ten at night (laughter). No official complaint had ever been made about the conduct of the dancers. Mr Joseph Heap, a restaurant keeper and member of the Town Council, objected to the noise from the music and dancing.'

This debate would continue on into the next century. On 4 June 1906, 'Dancing on Central Pier was a subject discussed at the Town Council this morning. The Town Clerk read the letters. The Free Church Council wrote that "The dancing carried out was not conducive to the best morals of the town". Despite the letters, the General Purposes Committee decided that dancing should be allowed until 1909.'

Admission for dancing and for entry into the hugely popular roller-skating rink, opened in 1909, was one halfpenny. One of the attractions of the pier was advertised in 1913 as 'Open Air Dancing above the Sea'.[21]

Harry Jacobs was a local man, born in 1888, who showed an early musical talent. By the time he was 20 he was already an experienced performer,

Postcard of Mr Harry Jacobs'
Orchestra, 1912.

playing the piano and leading a small band. As the postcard above indicates, his band would have been employed for the holiday season. Over the years, many different bands would have played for dancing on the pier.

The musicians in the photograph would have been assembled by Harry Jacobs in response to the requirements of their contract. An eighteen piece band would have been necessary for large crowds to hear the music in an open air environment.

Longridge Orchestral Band

THE first reference concerning a string band from Longridge came on 26 February 1887. 'The 1st Annual Co-operative Ball took place on Saturday evening in the Co-operative Hall, Berry Lane. The Longridge String Band, under the leadership of Mr J. Lovatt, efficiently performed a fine selection of music.'

The band were mentioned again on 14 January 1893: 'At the conclusion of the entertainment the hall was arranged for dancing, the first dances being allotted to the old folks, who tripped along in a merry fashion in "ye good old country dances" to the strains of the Longridge String Band.'

Another band in Longridge, attached to St Wilfred's Roman Catholic church, was reported in January 1891: 'The Ball was held in the Co-operative Hall, Berry Lane. The St Wilfred's String Band was in attendance and soon after eight o'clock the dancing commenced and was kept up with spirit till early the following morning.'

St Lawrence's C of E church in Longridge also had a string band around the same time. An account of 4 February 1893 records that 'Another of the Social Gatherings, the proceeds of which are devoted to the organ fund, was held in the Girls' School on Tuesday evening. After the entertainment, dancing followed to the music of the St Lawrence's String Band.'

James Turner (1863–1941) was an important figure in the development of string bands in Longridge. He had most probably been a member of the Longridge String Band before leading his own band. In 1898 the Congregational Bazaar in Longridge, had Mr Turner's String Band playing for their dance. Around this time it had become fashionable to rename bands using the term Orchestral and, in due course, Mr Turner's String Band became known as the Longridge Orchestral Band.

We know that as leader of the band, James played the fiddle, because he is mentioned in a later newspaper article of 29 April 1922: 'Mrs George Saunders (piano) and James Turner (violin), played for a dance at Whitechapel.'

James Turner's name appears within the name of the band when, on 17 February 1912, a report mentions 'The Annual Longridge Brass Band

Longridge Orchestral Band *c.*1912.[22]

Social took place on Thursday last with Turner's Orchestral Band. There was a presentation to Mr Pickup who had been the Brass Band secretary for 16 years. He was presented with a 100 day clock by the bandmaster, Mr Clayton.' (Jack Clayton can be seen in the photograph of Longridge Orchestral Band.)

James Turner's Orchestral Band continued to be regularly enlisted, playing at events in the Longridge area. On 11 November 1905 an article reveals that 'The 2nd Annual Ball in connection with the Longridge Cricket Club took place at the Longridge Co-operative Hall and the music was supplied by Mr Turner's Orchestral Band.'

The optionally named Longridge Orchestral Band appeared in a newspaper reference of 19 October 1912, when the *Preston Chronicle* reported that 'Dancing classes were formed at the Longridge Co-operative Hall under the auspice of Longridge Orchestral Band. There was a large turnout on Thursday night.'

Jack Willan (cornet), Jack Clayton (euphonium), Fred Young (flute and piccolo), Cecil Hothersall (double bass), Coupe brothers (fiddles), unknown (piano), Jim Woodruff (fiddle and picollo).[23]

Jack Clayton had been bandleader of the Longridge Brass Band and cornet player, Jack Willan had also been a member. Fred Young was the leader of the Whittingham Asylum Orchestra and Cecil Hothersall became leader of the St Wilfred's Orchestral Band.

Members of the Longridge Orchestral Band would also play in smaller musical combinations, depending on the size of the event. 'The Grimsargh farmers held a Social at the Assembly Rooms on Thursday. The date was brought forward so that several men who had been called-up could attend. Miss Woodruff (piano) and Messrs Carter and Coupe played violins.'

On 28 February 1914: 'The Co-operative Hall, Longridge was crowded on Saturday evening, when the 4th Annual Social in connection with Chapel Hill Football Club, took place. The Longridge Orchestral Band provided the music.'

From 14 November 1914: 'The Co-operative Society held a Party at the Longridge Assembly Rooms on Saturday evening. 500 attended for tea In spite of the unsettled conditions. There was a Concert arranged by the Manchester C.W.S. and afterwards dancing to the Longridge Orchestral Band conducted by Mr Coupe.'

In the years prior to the start of the First World War, the *Preston Guardian* printed photographs of Farmers' Ball Committee's from all parts of the county. The Annual Farmers' Ball was taken very seriously. On 17 January 1914 the *Preston Guardian* published a feature on that year's proceedings.

'The Co-operative Halls, Longridge, were tastefully decorated on Thursday evening, when the Annual Farmers' Ball was held and the event was as successful as previous years. About 250 persons attended from Longridge and the surrounding districts of Chipping, Thornley, Ribchester and Goosnargh. The chairman of the Ball Committee was Mr R. Nuttall of Ward Hall. The Longridge Orchestral Band played for dancing.'

Despite the outbreak of war, the band continued to play for dances. This item is from 27 November 1915: 'Clegg's Long Night with the Longridge Orchestral Band on Saturday night raised the sum of £6 7s. 6d. A total of 18,000 cigarettes, 200 quarter lbs of tobacco and 600 chocolate bars had been bought from R. Cross for dispatch to the troops.'

October 1917: 'There was a Clegg's Long Night, the first of the Season, at the Co-operative Hall with the Longridge Orchestral Band. There was a new dance, The Destiny Waltz, and £13 was raised out of a total of £227 0s. 1d. to date.'

Dances attracted a large number of people as this report from 16 February 1918 illustrates: 'St Wilfred's held their Annual Social and Dance at the Co-operative Hall on Tuesday. It was attended by 540 people with the Longridge Orchestral Band providing the music.'

The band continued to play throughout the 1920s. They were always busy, mainly playing at the large Longridge Co-operative Hall. On 15 January 1921: 'A Fancy Dress Ball held at the Longridge Co-operative

Blue plaque on the Longridge Co-operative building.

Hall with music provided by the Longridge Orchestral Band. The dances, in costume, included the Sir Roger De Coverley, an Old Fashioned Barn Dance, The Quadrilles and a novelty Foxtrot.'

The band also travelled to nearby villages. They remained much in demand, this event being reported on 5 February 1927: 'There was a Farmers' Ball at Grimsargh with 150 attending and music provided by the Longridge Orchestral Band.' In the same year, on 27 April: 'There was an Easter Social at Chipping, with Longridge Orchestral Band.'[24]

The final mention of the band was on 20 February 1930. 'The Longridge Orchestral Band organised a dance at the Longridge Co-operative Hall.'

LONGRIDGE ORCHESTRAL BAND.—
DANCE, CO-OPERATIVE HALL, SATURDAY,
October 4th, 7 to 11 p.m.   Admission 1/-.

CO-OP HALLS, Longridge.—Grand Dance
and Whist Drive, Saturday, November 2nd, 7 till
11 30. 1/-.   Late 'Buses.   Longridge Orchestral Band.

LEFT 3 October 1919.

RIGHT *Lancashire Daily Post*, 1 November 1929.

The author interviewed Jim McDowell during November 2010. His father had been in the Longridge Orchestral Band in the late 1920s. Jim was born in 1918 and joined the Longridge St Wilfred's Orchestra in 1934, aged 16.

The leader of St Wifred's Dance Band was Cecil Hothersall, who had also been in the Longridge Orchestral Band and played what Jim termed the Bass Fiddle. Apart from Cecil, the other instrumentalists were Jim on clarinet and fiddle, a piano accordionist, banjo-ukulele player and a drummer.

The orchestra played most Saturday nights in St Wilfred's Schoolroom. It cost 9*d.* to attend the dance, the proceeds going towards church funds.

The band also travelled to nearby villages. In November and December, 1937, there are two accounts of dances. On 14 November 1938: 'There was a Celebration Tea in connection with Grimsargh Football Club with dance music from St Wilfred's Band of Longridge.' Finally, on 3 December 1938: 'The St Wilfred's Orchestra provided the music for the Ball at Chipping.'

Whittingham Asylum String Band

WHITTINGHAM HOSPITAL was situated in the village of Goosnargh and was completed in 1873. It grew to be the largest mental hospital in the country. During its time, it had its own church, farms, railway, telephone exchange, post office, reservoirs, gas works, brewery, orchestra, brass band, ballroom and butchers.

There are a number of references of music from Whittingham in the *Preston Guardian*. The first of them, from 31 December 1881, mentions the Whittingham Asylum String Band playing for dancing when Whittingham Hospital held its Christmas Party. 'Twenty dances were played by a quartet from the excellent String Band of Whittingham Asylum. The music was played with spirit. The company, old and young, looked happy and the strains of "Sir Roger" wound up this happy reunion.'

The Whittingham musicians played in nearby Longridge on 4 February 1889, when 'the Whittingham Asylum String Band played at the 7th Annual Catholic Ball in the Co-operative Hall, Longridge'.

The asylum itself had a wonderful ballroom and held dances for the public. The *Preston Guardian* on 6 January 1900 has a report of a ball at Whittingham. 'The Attendants' and Nurses' Annual Ball took place at the Whittingham Asylum on Monday evening in the ballroom. The Asylum Orchestral Band under the conductorship of Mr Harry Turnbull went through an excellent programme of dance music.'

William Thomas Spain was born in London in 1864 and was the Asylum String Bandmaster during the first decade of the 1900s. The band consisted mainly of attendants at the hospital and had an unusually large collection of musicians. They would have had no problem creating enough volume for dancing.

The role of the orchestra must have been regarded as vital, an impression supported by the advertisement below, from *The Era* national newspaper. Most of the staff came from Goosnargh and the surrounding districts of

Whittingham Asylum String Band with their bandmaster, William Spain *c.*1905.

50

County Asylum, Whittingham, Preston.
WANTED, Male Attendants capable of Playing
Solo Cornet or Double Bass; also Bassoon.
Wages commence at £30 a-Year,
with Board, Lodging, Washing, and Uniform.
Apply to the SUPERINTENDENT,
giving full particulars.

WHITTINGHAM ASYLUM
}STRING BAND

Advertisement in *The Era*, 10 May 1890.

Longridge. It was said at the time that anyone who could play an instrument or who was a good cricketer was assured employment at the asylum. Fred Young, who was a flute and piccolo player in the Longridge Orchestral Band, was also leader of the Asylum Band in the 1920s.[25]

The Whittingham Band was also involved with the Whittingham and Goosnargh Festival. The start of the celebrations involved the crowning of the Festival Queen, which was followed by the band playing for children's morris and maypole dancing on the Green. The week following the Festival was the Annual Garden Party at the Vicarage where the band again played for traditional dances.[26]

The asylum held dances for the wider community. The following

The Whittingham Band *c*.1906/1907.

advertisement is for people in Preston who wished to attend the dance at Whittingham. Buses departed from the Red Lion Yard, Church Street, Preston.

On 2 January 1909: 'There was a Nurses and Attendants Ball at Whittingham Asylum and it took place in the Recreation Hall on New Year's Eve. The interior of the building had been lavishly decorated with palms and other foliage plants. The Asylum Orchestra, under the direction of Mr Spain, provided the music for dancing.'

Perhaps this article on 31 December 1910 explains how the band was used for dances. 'On Tuesday evening, the Attendants' Annual Supper took place and was followed by a dance, the music being supplied by a portion of the band under the conductorship of Mr Spain.'

The village of Barton organised a fund-raising event for the war effort. A 12 July 1918 account tells that 'a feature of the Fete was the "Barton Bank", a gaily decorated garden shelter in the decorated grounds. One of the attractions was the Whittingham Asylum Band, which played for dancing.'

The band continued after the First World War and there is an article from 31 December 1921 which reported that 'the Annual Patients' Ball was held in the Recreation Room of the County Asylum, Whittingham, on Monday afternoon. The Asylum Band provided the music for dancing.'

The hall was also used by other bands too. On 17 February 1923 'a successful social was held at Whittingham Hospital Recreation Hall on Monday. The music for dancing was supplied by Mr Frank David's Orchestra.'

WHITTINGHAM BALL.
'BUSES will leave T. Heskin's Red Lion Yard, Monday January, 1st at 7 p.m., for Whittingham Ball. Persons intending going please give their names in at the office.

Lancashire Daily Post, 1 January 1906.

Chipping String Band / Henpecked Club

CHIPPING is a small village in the rural Ribble Valley in an area known as the Forest of Bowland. By the end of the nineteenth century, industry included powered cotton mills, a foundry and a chair manufacturer. The Chipping String Band played in a similar area of the Forest of Bowland as the Winder Family Band from Wyresdale, on its northern border.

There are a number of references to the Chipping String Band in the *Preston Guardian*, the first being on 25 February 1899: 'THE ANNUAL

DANCE AT CHIPPING – The Annual Dance took place in the New School in the village; the local String Band played for the dancing.'

The village of Chipping celebrated Edward VII's coronation on 30 August 1902, when 'there was a Field Day and Sports. The Chipping String Band provided music for dancing during the Saturday afternoon.'

The band would have had to travel a distance of about ten miles when they appeared at Calder Vale near Garstang. On 3 January 1903 the newspaper reported that 'The Public Hall at Calder Vale was prettily decorated on New Year's Eve when a Ball took place. The company, which numbered between 70 and 80, danced to the music supplied by the Chipping String Band.'

James Clegg, famous for his Long Nights at the Longridge Co-operative Hall, appeared at an event that was reported on 9 January 1904. 'On New Year's Eve, the quaint village of Chipping held a most successful Sale of Work and a Dance. It was held in the New Brabbins School in Chipping. Jas. Clegg of Longridge gave several comic recitations and the Chipping String Band performed the dance music.'

The *Preston Guardian* of 11 November 1905 informs us that 'a dance took place at Brabbins School, Chipping, on Wednesday, having for its object the raising of funds for the Chipping String Band.'

Field Days or Club Days are annual fund-raising fetes or galas and are quite common in this area of Lancshire. On 22 June 1906: 'The Annual Fete held at Claughton, near Garstang, yesterday was the most successful of the series. In the evening, a dance was held in a large marquee and the Chipping String Band discoursed dance music.' The advertisement below is for a similar event two years later.

CLAUGHTON FIELD DAY, JUNE 25TH, 1908. By kind permission, and with the approval and support of W. FITZHERBERT-BROCKHOLES, Esq., J.P., C.A., D.L., this Premier Field Day will be held in the same place as last year, amid beautiful surroundings. CHIPPING BAND is again engaged. The Artistes are a Funny Lot. COUNTRY DANCE from 7 to 11 p.m. A popular event. The success of this Field Day is now public property. The Refreshments are

Preston Guardian, June 1908

During 1907 the band perfomed at Dunsop Bridge on 12 January 'The Farmers' Annual Ball was held in the village Reading Room. Dancing commenced at 8.30 p.m. to the strains of the Chipping String Band.' Later the same month they travelled to Garstang, when they played for the Oddfellows' Ball at the Institute.

An event to raise money for their funds took place on 16 November 1912. 'The Chipping String Band held their Annual Dance in the Parish Hall on Saturday evening, the event being greatly enjoyed. Mr William Nuttall, the secretary of the band, was in charge of arrangements. The proceeds were in aid of the band's funds.'

Prior to the war, on 3 January 1914, 'the Chipping branch of the Farmers' Union held their Annual Ball in the New School, Chipping, on New Year's Eve. Dancing continued until 4 o'clock, the Chipping String Band providing the music.'

The last reference using the term 'string band' was on 6 April 1918. 'Mrs Knowles of The Dairy, Chipping, organised a dance for the Soldiers' Fund which raised £8. The Chipping String Band provided the music for dancing.' After the First World War the band became known as the Chipping Orchestral Band.

On 24 December 1926, 'there was a dance at Chipping Oddfellows' Hall, organised by the Chipping Comforts and Welfare Committee for Preston Infirmary. The Chipping Orchestral Band provided the music.' 'Old habits dying hard' was proved true for some when on 13 March 1933 the musicians were still being described as a String Band. 'Two hundred members and friends of the Chipping Women's Institute entertained at the Open Night when a hot-pot supper was served. A social evening followed when the Chipping String Band played for dancing.'

The Henpecked Club

THE 'musicians' in the photograph, shown outside one of the Chipping mills, were known as the Chipping Henpecked Club. These clubs seem to have been quite common in nineteenth-century Lancashire and Yorkshire and continued until the 1930s.

The Talbot Hotel in Chipping was the home of the local 'Henpecked Club'. The club met annually on the day after Ascension Day. The participants elected a Mayor and then proceeded to visit every pub in the area.

There are a number of articles about these clubs in local newspapers. This is from the *Burnley Advertiser* on 4 August 1866. 'Last Saturday the Sabden Henpecked Club walked in procession. We understand that there were considerably over a hundred of them and that they were headed by a band of music. The foremost man carried a stag's horn and the rest bore various articles found in the household – mops, sweeping brushes, blacking and black lead brushes. We are informed that their place of meeting is at a "beershop" between Sabden and Padiham.'

Also in the *Burnley Advertiser* of 27 January 1872: 'The members of the Henpecked Husbands' Club of Mereclough, in Cliviger, sat down to an excellent supper at the Kettledrum Inn. The partakers, numbering about 37, having done ample justice to the old English roast beef and the other good things set before them, Mr Wilkinson Taylor, who is over eighty years, was called to the chair. A number of songs were sung including the "Henpecked Club" by William Walker. Numerous toasts and dancing followed; the most noticeable part of the latter being a contest between Procter, Stringer and Dean, to prove who was the best step-dancer.'

On 13 May 1899, the *Blackburn Standard* printed an article about the annual Great Harwood May Show. 'The procession started at Towngate and was composed of, first the fire brigade, then the Rishton Band and morris dancers from Whalley, then came the Celebrated Henpecked Club.'

In 1951, a *Lancashire Evening Post* article about 75-year-old Jack Barton, from nearby Ribchester village, describes how, on the day after 'Ribchester

Club Day', the harassed husbands or Henpecked Club would parade around the village carrying mops and brushes. They would visit all the establishments, including the village inns, where they would sing and dance to the music of the concertina.

Finally, this item appeared in the *Lancashire Evening Post* on 17 April 1933. 'HENPECKED HAVE THEIR ANNUAL DAY OF FREEDOM! – The Henpecked Club were this morning due to meet somewhere in the Calder Valley.'

BILSBORROW HENPECKED CLUB –
Christmas Dance, Bilsborrow School, 8 p.m.
December 23rd, 1930. Admission 1/-. Yale Band.

Advertisement in the *Lancashire Evening Post* of 13 November 1930.

Oswald Ainsworth's String Band (Horwich)

OSWALD AINSWORTH was born in Bury in 1871. He moved to Horwich, where he lived at 194 Crown Lane. He worked as a turner and fitter at the Horwich Locomotive Works of the Lancashire and Yorkshire Railway Company, the largest employer in the town.

All the following articles are from the *Horwich Chronicle*. On 26 October 1901: 'The Annual Concert and Dance promoted by the Horwich Industrial Co-operative Society was held in the large hall of the Mechanic's Institute. The Horwich Quadrille Band, under the conductorship of Mr Oswald Ainsworth, provided the music for dancing.'

On 14 February 1903: 'The large hall at the Mechanics Institute presented a gay appearance on Wednesday evening, when the Second Annual Ball in connection with the Conservative Association was held. Mr Oswald Ainsworth's Band provided the music for dancing.'

On 2 February 1907: 'A very enjoyable dance, promoted by the members of the National School, was held in the Church Hall on Wednesday evening. The music was supplied by Mr O. Ainsworth's Band.'

In the same year, on 9 November 1907: 'The dance in connection with the Railway Men's Institute was held in the Mechanics' Club on Friday evening. About 70 persons were present. Mr O. Ainsworth's Band provided the music.'

Advertisement for a 'Select Coronation Dance', Horwich, 1902.

CENTRAL HALL, HORWICH.

A SELECT

Coronation Dance

Will be held in the above Hall,

On Thursday, June 26th, 1902.

Mr. AINSWORTH'S STRING BAND will be in attendance.

M.C.—Mr. R. NIGHTINGALE.

DANCING from 8 to 12.   Tickets—SIXPENCE.

On 14 November 1908: 'The Annual Dance in connection with Horwich R.M.I. Football Club took place on Saturday evening in the Mechanic's Institute. Messrs Ainsworth's and Harper's Band provided the music, dancing continued until midnight.' An article in the *Horwich Chronicle* on 30 January 1909 mentions Oswald as a violinist and that he was also involved with the Horwich Amateur Dramatic Society.

On 6 February 1909: 'The Horwich section of the Clarion Cycling Club, held their Annual Social and Dance in the Assembly Room of the Horwich Reform Club. Mr Ainsworth's Band provided the music.'

Finally, on 27 February 1909: 'HORWICH LIBERALS – The Annual Social, Concert and Dance promoted by members of the Horwich Reform Club, was held on Wednesday evening. Messrs Harper and Ainsworth's Quadrille Band supplied the music for dance.'

Gregson's String Band (Kirkham)

GREGSON'S STRING BAND was based in Kirkham and as the photograph indicates, included four generations of the Gregson family. Thomas Gregson is on the front row, holding the cornet. He also played in the Kirkham Brass Band.

In May 2010 Belle Gregson of Freckleton contacted the local newspaper after an appeal for more information about the band. The man who is on

Gregson's String Band, *c*.1910.[28]

the back row, far right, is her father-in-law John Gregson and the two men on John's right are his brothers Billy and Bob. The man immediately in front of John on the front row is another brother, George. Their father is the man on the left of the photograph, with the cello.

The following articles are from the *Preston Guardian* and all dances take part in small villages around Kirkham.

7 January 1905: 'On Saturday evening a dance took place at Warton School, attended by about 50 persons. The music was played by Mr Gregson.'

6 January 1906: 'DANCING AT ESPRICK – On Monday evening, the Annual Tea Party and Dance in connection with Esprick School was held. About 130 persons sat down to tea. Dancing soon commenced to the strains of Gregson's String Band.'

13 February 1909: 'On Friday evening a Social was held at the Weeton National School. The arrangements were in the hands of Mr Albert Threlfall from Weeton Post Office. Dancing began shortly after eight o'clock to music supplied by Mr. Gregson's Band.'

Finally, on 26 November 1910: 'The Annual Treales Tea Party took place on Thursday evening. After tea, dancing took place to the music provided by Mr Gregson's String Band from Kirkham.'

Samuel Hobson's Band (Rawtenstall)

SAMUEL HOBSON was born at Idle, in Yorkshire, in 1844. He married Margaret Siddall from Rawtenstall in 1864 and by 1881 they were living in Rawtenstall, in the Rossendale Valley. His occupation was described in that year's census return as a Master Stone Mason, employing 27 hands. They had two daughters, Emily and Ada and a son Frederick.

A report in the *Blackburn Standard* of 1 July 1876 shows that he was involved with the Independent Order of Rechabites, when he was recorded as being present at their meeting in Bacup. 'Spirited addresses in favour of temperance were delivered by the chairman, Bro S. Hobson, Rawtenstall. The addresses were agreeably interspersed with selections of vocal and instrumental music.'

The *Burnley Gazette* on 13 May 1903 reports on a meeting in Nelson. 'Brother Samuel Hobson of Rawtenstall related his life story in an interesting narrative. He interspersed his remarks with music on several instruments.'

Samuel Hobson's Band, *c.*1910.[29]

There is a mention of dancing in the following report from the *Rossendale Free Press* of 2 January 1904. 'It was with a two-fold object that the Cinderella Committee arranged a Tea and Social on Christmas Eve. A capital tea was provided in Mr S. Hobson's room, Holmfield. After the tea, Mr Hobson presided over the social in his usual genial manner. Dancing and games filled up the programme.'

In the same newspaper on 6 January 1912: 'The committee of the Rechabites held the annual Tea and Social at Cunliffe's Restaurant, Burnley Road. After tea, they made their way to Bro S. Hobson's rooms at Holmfield Yard for a social.'

The Clowbridge Orchestra

THE small village of Clowbridge lies between Rawtenstall and Burnley. The Clowbridge Orchestra was connected to the Clowbridge Baptist Chapel, which is only two miles from Goodshaw Chapel and the Larks of Dean musicians.

The Clowbridge Orchestra.

There are a number of references in the *Burnley News* regarding the orchestra. On 21 April 1906, the paper reported that 'On Good Friday, Saturday and Easter Monday, a Bazaar was held in the Clowbridge Baptist Church Schoolroom, with the view of clearing off the debt of £400. Instrumental selections were given by the Clowbridge Orchestra.'

It appears that Clowbridge Orchestra musicians also played for dancing as the two following articles indicate when musicians are named in both events.

10 March 1917: 'The workpeople of Messrs W. Landless and Sons, Clowbridge Mills, on Tuesday held a Concert and Dance in the Conservative Club at Crawshawbooth. The proceeds are to be divided in the form of parcels amongst those of the employees now serving in the Army or Navy. An orchestra with Mrs W. Shutt and Mr J. R. Farnworth as pianists; Mrs Ingham, Messrs C. Walker, E. Livesey, C. Duckworth as violinists; Mr E Tattersall, cornet player; Mr R. Taylor, 'cello and Mr E. Nuttall, bass fiddle, played for dancing at the close of the concert.'

After the First World War, on 24 December 1919: 'A large congregation assembled in the Baptist Chapel on Sunday evening, when portions of Handel's Messiah were rendered by the combined choirs of Clowbridge Baptist Chapel and Providence U.M.C., Loveclough assisted by the Clowbridge Orchestra. The instrumentalists in the orchestra were; 1st violins, Mrs Crowther, Messrs C. Duckworth and J. Nuttall; 2nd violins,

Messrs C. Walker, J. Eastwood and W. Tattersall; 'cello, Mr R. Taylor; double bass, Mr E. Nuttall; clarionette, Mr A. Cooper; organists, Mr W. Landless and Mr J.R. Farnworth.'

An article about a concert at the Clowbridge Baptist School identifies the leader of the orchestra. On 31 January 1920: 'The programme opened with a march, The Gallant 55th, a composition by Mr J.R. Farnworth, conductor of the Clowbridge Orchestra.'

Stanhill String Band

STANHILL village lies on the moors above Oswaldtwistle, to the east of Blackburn. James Hargreave, inventor of the 'spinning jenny' multi-spindle spinning frame, was born at nearby Knuzden Brook in 1720. His invention, in 1764, improved the early mechanisation of cotton spinning.

The Stanhill String Band was connected to the Methodist church in the village and was renowned for its involvement in what were known as the Stanhill Sermons. 'A time-honoured custom, celebrated every year on the first Sunday in May, is the Charity Sermons at Stanhill, really the Sunday School Anniversary known far and wide as Stanhill Fair. The Schoolchildren parade the village in their best attire, sing in front of Stanhill Hall and at various points in the village, accompanied by a string band – surely reminiscent of the days when the cello, flute and violin were the accompaniment of old time Psalm and sacred song.'[30]

In a *Lancashire Evening Post* article of 8 May 1937, a former musician at the church was about to celebrate his Golden Wedding Anniversary. 'Mr and Mrs Ralph Smalley of Falls Farm Cottage, Stanhill Lane, Oswaldtwistle, will tomorrow observe the 50th year of their wedding.'

'They were married at Stanhill Methodist Church on Saturday 9 May 9th 1887. Cotton mill operative, colliery worker, farmer and shop assistant, Mr. Smalley retired five years ago at the age of 67. He was Choirmaster at Stanhill Methodist Church in the year of his marriage and for fifty years he has formed one of the band musicians who play at various points in the village for the Stanhill "Sermons" on the first Saturday in May. He is a violin and cello player.'

At Knuzden Free Methodist Church, just one mile from the Stanhill Methodist Church, a similar band existed. Miles Nightingale, born in

The Stanhill Sermons 1900 – note the
young lads holding sheets of music.[31]

First Sunday in May, Stanhill
String Band at Stanhill,
Oswaldtwistle on 5 May 1907.

The Stanhill String Band, *c.*1909.

The 1912 Stanhill Sermons
at Stanhill Hall.[33]

Horwich in 1826, became a 'Spinning Master' at Knuzden Brook Mill. In his autobiography he describes his involvement in establishing a band within his church.[32]

'In June 1893, I commenced a string band to be called The Knuzden Free Methodist String Band. Sixteen young men joined the band. My object in commencing the string band was to find our young men something to do and keep them at school. I am pleased to say that up to present, it has not only been a way of keeping our young men at school, but a means bringing others to the school who did not attend before the formation of the band. Their parents also seem to have more interest in the place.'

'I have written over 100 pieces of music for the different instruments of the band. The first violin five times over, second violin twice, for I was anxious to give them all the encouragement I could. I have written 1451 hymn tunes into books which I have presented to the trustees for the use of the band and choir. These tunes have been written several times over so as to give sufficient copies for the players and singers.'

The leader of the band in the 1912 photograph is Charles Hyatt, second from the right on the back row and extreme left in the 1909 photograph. The men in the straw boaters seem detached from the main group of musicians. One has a tambourine and another has a pair of 'bones'.

Huncoat String Band

THERE is a reference to this church band in the *Burnley Express* of 8 March 1879. 'A Public Tea Party was held in the Mount Zion Baptist Chapel on Saturday last. After tea a service of song entitled "Joseph" was given, assisted by the Huncoat String Band. The instrumentalist were; 1st violin, Messrs J. Clarke and J. Hudson; 2nd violin, Messrs R. Hudson and T. Nuttall; viola, Mr W.C. Pollard; cello, Mr B.T. Westwell; bass, Mr G. Clarke; cornet, Mr T. Moore and harmonium, Mr J. Clarke.'

There is an account of a procession in the *Lancashire Evening Post* of 10 June 1935. 'Whit Monday processions in Huncoat, may not have the same hold as in the days when the banner was floating over the gates of Huncoat Baptist Chapel, but they retain old world characteristics. Fiddle and flute are still played by musicians as the processionists pause at different parts of the village to sing their hymns. In many instances these musicians have played in the processions for a greater part of their lives.'

Again in the *Lancashire Evening Post*, 17 May 1937: 'Grouped in Higher Gate, Huncoat, Accrington, cellists, fiddlers and other string and wind instrumentalists played at noon today in traditional fashion for the singing by the united Sunday schools of the village.'

'The glorious sunshine added to the disappointment of Mr George Barnes, a veteran Baptist cello player who was unable to join in this year's celebrations after walking 75 times in the Whit Monday procession and playing in 62 of them. Mr John. W. Pollard, an 82-year-old Methodist, who

has been walking since the age of three, and has been absent only three or four times, took part. Some of the musicians had long records with the Methodists. Mr Sam Howarth, cellist and Mr Herbert Nichol, a violinist, were making their 48th appearance and Mr Ted Haworth, bass, who has been playing since he was 11, was walking for his 54th year.'

Darwen Orpheus String Band

A N article in the *Darwen News* of 16 November 1904 sheds light on the formation of the Darwen Orpheus String Band. It concerned the death of Joseph Hindle, a violinist, cornet player and prominent musician in Darwen for over thirty years.

'Joseph Hindle was the original tutor of the Co-operative Servants' Band, of which the present Orpheus Band is really the outcome.' The first reference of the band playing for dancing was on 10 December 1892. 'On Tuesday the Annual Ball in connection with the Darwen Central Conservative Club was held at the Public Hall. Music was provided by the Orpheus String Band.'

Many of the balls and dances in Darwen were held at the Co-operative Hall, which was the largest dance venue in the town. From an account of 18 November 1893: 'On Tuesday the Annual Ball in connection with the Darwen division of the Liberal League, was held at the Co-operative Hall. There was a large attendance, which included most of the prominent Liberals in the town. Music was provided by the Orpheus Band.'

5 November 1898: 'The 5th Annual Ball in connection with the Darwen Cycling Club was held on Tuesday night in the Co-operative hall. The Orpheus Band discoursed music for dancing, which was kept up to the small hours of Wednesday morning. The programme included: Preliminary valse, valse, lancers, schottische, polka, two-step and the barn dance.'

4 June 1899: 'Last Tuesday evening, at the invitation of Mr Romney Duckworth, the Darwen Orpheus Band, 12 in number, attended the Workhouse and gave an Instrumental Concert, which was much appreciated by the inmates. At the close Rev Wales proposed a vote of thanks, seconded by Mr Catterall, which was carried, amid loud cheers. Mr Walmsley, the conductor, suitably replied on behalf of the band.'

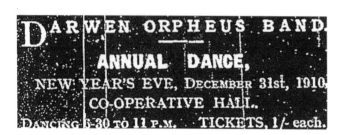

Advertisement for Darwen Orpheus Band Annual Dance.

6 October 1900: 'On Saturday a Tea Party and Ball was held in the Co-operative Hall, Darwen under the auspices of the local branch of the Operative Cotton Spinners' Association. There was a capital attendance and after an excellent tea had been partaken of, the rest of the evening was spent in dancing. The music was supplied by the Orpheus Band under the leadership of Mr Robert Walmsley.'

Finally, a report of the above dance appeared in the *Darwen Advertiser* on 6 January 1911. 'The Annual Dance organised by the Orpheus Band was held in the Co-operative Hall on New Year's Eve. The band, under the conductorship of Mr Robert Walmsley, rendered a very fine programme of music.'

Pickup Bank String Band

PICKUP BANK is a hamlet, two miles to the east of Darwen and near to the village of Hoddlesden. There had been a brass band at Pickup Bank since 1864 and the following article, from the *Blackburn Standard* of 16 August 1879, describes the band playing for dancing. 'HODDLESDEN

FAIR AND SPORTS – On Saturday last, the 6th Annual Fair and Sports were held in a field behind the Ranken Arms. At the conclusion of the sports, the Pickup Bank Brass Band under the leadership of Mr Thomas Harwood played for dancing.'

Thomas Harwood was born in 1837. His father, James, had been a handloom weaver at Pickup Bank. In the 1901 census he was recorded as being a farmer living at Scholes Fold, Pickup Bank, but he had also been an 'overlooker' in the local cotton mill.

It is quite possible that the members of the church involved in the following article were actually members of the string band. On 26 June 1886, a report declares that 'a Cantata was repeated by special request at the Independent Chapel, Yates and Pickup Bank, by the chapel choir and assisted by friends. The vocalists were: Leader, Mr John Harwood; harmoniumist, Mr Charles Harwood; soprano Miss Betsy Harwood; tenor, Mr Thomas Harwood; violins, Messrs E. Grime and A. E. Duckworth; double bass, Mr Councillor Wardley (Darwen), assisted by members of the Pickup Brass Band.'

The first reference to the Pickup Bank String Band itself was on 6 January 1900 in the *Blackburn Standard*. 'In connection to the Hoddlesden Conservative Club, the Annual At Home was held last Saturday night in the Co-operative Hall. The Pickup Bank String Band played for dancing and the MCs were Messrs Thomas Ellis and Arthur Irwin.'

There also appeared an article about a fundraising event for the Pickup Bank Congregational Church. Dated 10 November 1905, it says that 'During the evening the Pickup Bank String Band provided the music for dancing.'

Again, on 9 October 1909: 'A Dance was held under the auspices of the Pickup Bank Subscription Brass Band, in the Hoddlesden Co-operative Hall on Tuesday evening. Mr J.J. Harwood was the pianist'. It is quite likely that he was the pianist from the string band and a link to the former leader of the brass band.

An article from 25 February 1910 covers an event organised by the Hoddlesden Liberal Club. 'On Saturday evening, there was a large attendance at the Hoddlesden Co-operative Hall, when the Annual Tea Party of the Liberal Club was held and was followed by a Concert and Dance. The Pickup Bank String Band rendered the following programme of dance music: Preliminary valse, "Spirit of Love"; barn dance, "In the moonlight"; lancers, "Merry

Advertisement for Hoddlesden Liberal Club Subscr. Tea Party & Dance.

HODDLESDEN LIBERAL CLUB.

Subscription TEA PARTY, ENTERTAINMENT AND DANCE, in the CO-OPERATIVE HALL, HODDLESDEN, on SATURDAY, DEC. 18th, 1909. Entertainment by our Local Friends. Accompanist, J. YATES. Chairman, MR. THOS. HARWOOD. Pickup Bank String Band. Tea at 4-30. p.m., prompt. Entertainment 7. Dancing 9 till 11-50. Tickets 1/- each; under 13 years, 9d. Entertainment and Dance only, 9d. No Tickets sold for Tea after 6-45. A MEAT TEA provided. I. WOOD, Sec.

widow"; valeta, "Happy lovers"; two-step, "Coon's Parade"; lancers "Waltz dream"; esperano, "Original"; valse, "Merry Widow"; lancers, "Balmoral"; valeta, "Royal Court Ball"; schottische, "Dancer's Delight"; valse, "Venus on Earth"; lancers, "Old England"; and valse "Laughing Eyes".'

The band also promoted their own dances, this from 9 Friday December 1910. 'The Annual Ball of the Pickup Bank String Band was held in the Hoddlesden Co-operative Hall on Saturday evening. An excellent programme of music was rendered and the MCs for the evening were J. Yates, W. Woodcock and J. Walsh.'

Finally, on 21 February 1913. 'On Saturday last a successful Tea Party followed by a Concert and Dance was held in the Hoddlesden Co-operative Hall, in aid of funds for the erection of a Liberal Club in the village. The concert was provided by the Darwen Lyric Quartette Party and dancing provided by the Pickup Bank String Band.'

An interesting article appeared in the *Darwen Advertiser* on 11 May 1983, in which readers were asked to suggest why the Rosins Public House was so named. Phoebe Townsend, an 89-year-old relative of the original owner responded. 'The pub on Treacle Row, Pickup Bank was originally called

PICKUP BANK STRING BAND.

A GRAND BALL

Will be held in the **Hoddlesden Co-operative Hall,** on SATURDAY, MARCH 4th, 1911. M.C.'s: Messrs. J. YATES, J. WALSH, and G. W. WOODCOCK. Dancing from 7 till 11. Tickets, 6d. each. G. DUCKWORTH, Sec.

Darwen Advertiser, 4 March 1911.

Hoddlesden Co-operative Hall, now the Conservative Club

the Duke of Wellington and was used as a practice venue for the Pickup Bank String Band. A young lad called John was constantly sent to Darwen for replacement rosin for the violin bows and eventually the pub gained the name Rosins.'

Mr C.H. Byers' Band (Wigan)

THE photograph of Byers' Band includes two clarinets, a double bass, a trombone, two cornets, a flute, seven violins, a piano, a cello and drums. This seems a large number of musicians, but it would be a necessary configuration for any large dances where volume was important. The photograph is probably of an augmented band, suitable for the much larger events.

Byers' Band, *c*.1905.[35]

The first reference to the band was in the *Wigan Observer* on 28 January 1905. 'The interior of the Drill Hall, Wigan, presented a charming picture on Friday night, where the Mayor and Mayoress of Wigan gave a Dance to a large number of unmarried folk. This is known as the Senior Dance and attracted 800 people. Mr C.H. Byers' Band supplied the music. The dances included: polkas, waltzes, the lancers, barn dances and the valeta.' The next article on the same page reports on the Mayor and Mayoress's Dance for Juveniles. 'This too was a most enjoyable occasion. Mr Byers' Band discoursed the music and dancing began at 7 o'clock.'

The next two reports show that the band also played in much smaller venues in villages near Wigan. On 13 January 1906, an article mentioned the following local event. 'St Mark's Cricket Club, Pemberton, held their Annual Dance on New Year's Eve in the Newtown School. Dancing was indulged in to the strains of Mr C.H. Byers' Band, until three o' clock on Tuesday morning. The party then dispersed after singing Auld Lang Syne.'

Also in Pemberton, on 26 October 1907, a similar event was reported. 'The 3rd Annual Tea and Social under the auspices of Pemberton St. John's Young Mens' Bible class was held on Saturday week in the Large School. Mr C.H. Byers' Band discoursed an excellent selection of music and the dancing continued until 10 o' clock.'

Albert Porter's Quadrille Band (Rochdale)

ALBERT PORTER was born in Rochdale in 1876 and his family came from the Castleton area of the town. In 1901 he was living at Broomfield Square, Rochdale and his profession was given as a 'brass finisher'. By 1911, he was living at 96 Hare Street, Rochdale.

The *Rochdale Observer* of 8 December 1909 reports that 'The 10th Annual Ball promoted by the Rochdale Infirmary Workmen's Committee was held on Saturday evening in the Assembly Room of Rochdale Town Hall. Between 350 and 400 persons were present. Music for dancing was supplied by Mr Albert Porter's Orchestra.'

A band for such a prestigious event would have probably been augmented by extra musicians, so as to provide enough volume for such a large venue with so many dancers. (The photograph of Byers' Orchestra, Wigan, shows

Albert Porter's Quadrille
Band, c.1908[36]

the range of instruments and number of musicians used in an augmented band.)

The term 'quadrille band' was unusual at the time of the band photograph, as it had been replaced by 'string band', 'orchestra' or 'orchestral band'. The instrumental composition of these bands was similar and this particular photograph shows a classic line up of double-bass or bass-fiddle, two fiddles, cornet, clarinet, flute and piano.

Note the sign at the back of the stage to indicate the next dance. Newspaper reports of many of these events would mention the names of the Master of Ceremonies for the evening. Their position would be to compare the evening and announce the list of dances; the audience would already know how to do the dances.

Richard Snape's String Band (Wheelton)

RICHARD SNAPE was born in Wheelton in 1864. He was a cotton spinner at Peter Todd's Victoria Mill in Wheelton and lived on Meadow Street in the village.

All references are from the *Chorley Guardian*. The first is on 23 January 1886.

'The St. Mary's Catholic Ball was held at the Railway Hotel, Leyland.

The room was beautifully decorated and full of people. Dancing was to Mr Snape's String Band from Wheelton and continued until two o'clock.'

The following year, on 26 February 1887, they were termed a quadrille band when they played at a canalside pub. 'WHITTLE SPRINGS FOOTBALL CLUB – The 3rd Annual Concert and Ball in connection with this club was held on Monday evening in the room of the Navigation Inn, near Whittle Springs. Dancing commenced at 9 o'clock and every credit must go to Wheelton Quadrille Band for the excellent music they so ably rendered. They terminated the proceedings by playing Auld Lang Syne followed by God save the Queen.'

In February 1889 the *Chorley Standard* reported 'HEAPEY BUSY BEE CO-OPERATIVE SOCIETY – The Annual Tea Party took place in St Paul's School, Wheelton. After the songs, the remainder of the evening was spent dancing to the strains of the Wheelton String Band.' This was an event that they played for on a number of occasions.

In a report of 7 June 1890 they were again referred to as a quadrille band. 'MARRIAGE AT WHEELTON – There was much pleasant excitement in the neighbourhood of Wheelton on Wednesday last. This was the marriage of Miss Margaret Sarah Jackson, eldest daughter of Dr Edward Jackson of Rye Bank, Wheelton, to the Rev. Louis Arthur Bellhouse. In the evening a Party was given in a large marquee erected on the lawn. Subsequently there was a Ball, the music being provided by Mr Snape's Wheelton Quadrille Band.'

From an article dated 27 February 1892 the band appeared at the Howard Arms Hotel, a venue that had hosted dances and balls since it opened in the 1840s. 'BALL AT WHITTLE SPRINGS – On Wednesday evening a Tea Party and Ball took place at the Howard Arm's Hotel, Whittle Springs. The ballroom, which was crowded with dancers, was beautifully decorated. The music was supplied by the Wheelton String Band.'

18 October 1892: 'On Saturday evening, the Annual Ball in aid of funds for the Whittle-le-Woods Cricket Club was held in St. John's School, Whittle-le-Woods. The Wheelton String Band provided the music for dancing.'

The last reference to the Wheelton String Band was on 18 October 1902. 'The Annual Ball, in aid of funds for the Whittle-le-Woods Cricket Club, was held in St John's School. The Wheelton String Band provided the music.'

It seems that around this time Richard Snape started a band with his sons. In 1905, there was a social for St Chad's Catholic church in Whittle-le-Woods. 'The members of the St Chad's Club sat down to a knife and fork

Wheelton Council School,
now the Village Hall.

tea at the Red Cat Inn. Mr R. Snape's String Band played a selection of music. Mr Jackson played a solo on the flageolet.'

A report from 6 January 1912 declared that 'On Saturday evening, the St Chad's Church Annual Dance took place at the Whittle Springs Hotel. The large assembly room had been prettily decorated for the occasion. Dancing commenced at 6 o'clock to the strains of Mr Snape's Band.'

An extract about the annual Busy Bee Co-operative gathering in 1913 informs its readers that 'The Heapey Busy Bee Co-Operative Society Limited held their Annual Soiree at the Wheelton Council School on Saturday. Dancing was enjoyed under the guidance of Messrs R. Jolly and F. Rigby. Messrs Snape and Sons' Band provided the music.'

7 February 1914: 'The first Dance arranged in connection with the Wheelton and District Liberal Association took place in the Council School on Saturday evening. Dancing followed to the strains of R. Snape and Sons' String Band.'

Richard Snape had three sons, Sylvester, Richard Staines and Leo, who were all cotton spinners in Peter Todd's mill. Richard Staines Snape, clarinet player in the band was injured in the First World War in 1916. He had been a stretcher bearer and member of his regimental band. The string band continued after the war with Leo (piano), Sylvester (violin) and Richard Staines (clarinet). They would often play at the local Whittle Springs Hotel, a sizeable establishment, and became the resident band there. Richard Staines lived at Gorse Hall, where his father lived with his second wife. The second Mrs Snape had previously been a teacher at nearby St. Chad's School.[37]

The final reference to the band was their appearance at a fund-raising event for their church. Published on 22 October 1921, the article stated that 'A Dance was held in the ballroom of the Whittle Spring's Hotel in aid of St. Chad's Roman Catholic Church Club. Mr R. Snape's Orchestra provided the music for dancing.'

James Titherington's Band (Colne)

THERE is an interesting article about the Titherington family in the *Colne Times* from 1 March 1963. It says that 'The Titherington Family of Colne has a remarkable musical record. James Titherington joined the Colne Orchestra in 1896, just after it was formed.' A 1903 reference confirms that he played clarinet. The article goes on to say, 'His son, James Titherington junior, has played percussion in the same orchestra for forty years and his sister Kathleen Phelps is the principal cellist.'

James Titherington senior was also the leader of his own dance band in the Colne area of East Lancashire. On 27 November 1903 the local newspaper reported that 'The Annual Tea Party promoted by the tacklers of Colne was held on Saturday at the Co-operative Hall, Colne [a tackler supervised the running of the looms in the cotton mills]. Mr J. Titherington's Band played the music for dancing.'

James Titherington's Band, *c.*1907.[38]

The following week, a report details another event at which the band was involved. 'In the Co-operative Hall on Saturday, the members of Messrs S. Smith and Sons Sick Club held their 3rd Annual knife and fork Tea Party and Social. There was an attendance of 300 persons and J. Titherington's Band provided the music for dancing.'

From an item dated 20 April, 1904, readers learnt that 'On Saturday, the sixteenth Annual Tea and Social in connection with the Colne Centre for the St. John Ambulance Association, took place in the Co-operative Hall, Colne. Mr Titherington's Band provided the music for dancing.'

Finally, from 7 March 1906: 'The employees of Messrs Radcliffe's Skipton Road Mill, Colne, held their Annual Tea and Social at the Colne Co-operative Hall on Saturday. There were about 200 present. Titherington's Band played for dancing.'

Mr Mayor's Walmer Bridge String Band

JOHN MAYOR was born at Much Hoole in 1859. In 1901, he was living only a short distance away in Hall Lane, Longton. He was a schoolmaster at Walmer Bridge School.

All the following references to Mr Mayor and his band were gleaned from the *Preston Guardian*, beginning with the first article to mention the band, published on 21 November 1908. 'The Annual Social connected to the Longton and District Agricultural Society was held in the Longton Schoolrooms. In the evening, Mr Mayor's String Band from Walmer Bridge played for dancing.'

20 February 1909: 'A Rose Social and Dance was held at Longton Parish Church Schoolrooms. The dance music was provided by Mr Mayor's String Band.' Also, a week later, 'The Longton Football Club held a dance at St. Andrew's Schoolroom. Mr Mayor's String Band played for dancing.'

20 November 1909: 'The Walmer Bridge String Band gave its first winter Soirée in the Walmer Bridge Schoolroom on Saturday. There was a good attendance and a very pleasant evening was enjoyed.'

14 December 1912: 'A Social and Dance, in aid of the Church Missionary Society, was held at the Hoole C.of E. School on Saturday. Dancing was later indulged in to the strains of the Walmer Bridge String Band, under the direction of Mr Mayor.'

The following week, on 21 December: 'An enjoyable Social was held in the Walmer Bridge Schoolroom on Saturday evening. The event was to raise funds for a screen for the schoolroom and was organised by Mr Mayor (schoolmaster). A large number of people indulged in dancing to the music of the Walmer Bridge String Band, conducted by Mr Mayor.'

It can be reasonably assumed that John Mayor led the band by playing the fiddle. An account of 7 February 1914 reveals that 'A concert was held in the Primitive Methodist School in Walmer Bridge. Mr J. Mayor gave a violin solo.'

An article printed on 22 February 1919, illustrates the close relationship between the village dance band and the village brass band. 'Walmer Bridge is probably unique for a township of its size in the possession of two local bands, a string band and a brass band. The former has been in existence for nearly 20 years. During the past four years both bands have been in great demand by neighbouring townships in connection with efforts on behalf of the war. In this way they have rendered much useful service. In appreciation of this work the ladies of Walmer Bridge, Hoole and Longton organised a Social and Dance on Saturday evening on behalf of the two bands. The Schoolroom had been lent for the night by Messrs Crowden and Grierson. There was a very large gathering, charabancs having brought people from Leyland, Penwortham, Bretherton and Tarleton. The bands were in attendance and played for dancing. They raised almost £20.'

5 November 1919: 'A fundraising Dance in aid of St. Mark's Football Team was held in Longton. Mr J. Mayor's String Band (Walmer Bridge) played for dancing.'

The final reference to the band appeared on 29 October 1921. 'The members of the Hoole Institute held their first Dance of the season in the Club on Saturday evening, when there was a fair attendance. The Walmer Bridge String Band played for dancing.'

Henry Wilson's Band (Long Preston)

HENRY WILSON'S BAND came from the Craven district of Yorkshire, on the eastern fringes of Lancashire, edging the Forest of Bowland. They played in villages in Yorkshire, Lancashire and the old county of Westmorland. Henry Wilson, the leader of the band, said that he had played in every village from Grassington and Hawes down to Chatburn and Slaidburn.

There are many references to the band to be found in the *Lancaster Guardian*. The 23 January 1904 edition carried a piece recording that 'The Hellifield Athletic Association held its Ball in the Black Horse Assembly Room, Long Preston, on Friday, when forty persons attended. Dancing was kept up till 3 a.m. to the strains of Messrs Wilson's Band.'

On 2 January 1909: 'The Annual Ball was held in the Giggleswick Reading Rooms on Christmas Day. Dancing was kept up till 5 a.m. to the strains of Wilson's Band.' One can imagine that each musician would require considerable stamina to play for so long before having then to undertake their journey home.

26 February 1910: 'A successful Social on behalf of the local Liberal Association was held on Saturday in the Long Preston Mechanics' Institute. After the concert, dancing was kept up until three o'clock in the morning. Wilson's Band provided the music for dancing.'

25 February 1911: 'The Long Preston Football Club held a social in the Endowed School on Friday, when 168 guests assembled. Mr H. Wilson's Band provided the music for dancing.'

Later the same year, on 30 December: 'A thoroughly enjoyable Ball was held by the Bachelors in the Golden Lion Hotel, Settle, on Tuesday, when 52 persons attended. Dancing was kept up into the early hours to the strains of Mr Wilson's (Long Preston) Band.'

There are many reports from after the war. This one is from 5 November 1921: 'The Settle Cricket Club held its annual ball in the Victoria Hall, Settle. Mr H. Wilson's Full Band provided the music for dancing.'

In November 1950, the *Dalesman* magazine published an article by William Mitchell about Henry Wilson and his band. The interview with Henry shows his passion for playing music for dancing and gives a fascinating insight into how the band operated. He played continuously from the early 1900s until the time of the article, with breaks only during the two wars. When not involved with his playing commitments, he was the village blacksmith in Settle.[39]

Henry (Harry) Wilson was born in Settle in 1885 and moved at some point to Long Preston. He first became interested in playing for dances as a youth of 14, when he attended a dance at the Reading Room in Stainforth. The band comprised a violin and flute, as there were few pianos around at the time. A local band known as Kit Graham's Band did use a piano, which they took with them on a flat cart and would charge 15 shillings for an evening which would often continue on until 2 a.m. There is an account which mentions Kit Graham's Band, taken from the *Lancaster Guardian* of 15 November 1913. 'The Eldbroth Supper and Ball was held in the Austwick

The Wilson Family Band, *c*.1905.

Public Hall on Saturday. Graham's Band (Settle) provided the music for dancing.'

Another dance that Henry remembered was in Hellifield, where his uncle was playing the violin. His uncle asked if he would like to try accompanying him on the piano and afterwards he decided to assemble a family band. Henry played the flute, his sisters Dorothy and Kate played fiddle and piano, his father George played double-bass and his uncle Robert the fiddle.

The musicians in the photograph are, left to right: George Wilson, Robert Wilson (who was a joiner at Hellifield), Miss Dorothy Wilson, Henry Wilson and Miss Kate Wilson. The photograph was taken during a garden party at Halton Place, Halton West (between Hellifield and Gisburn). The Yorke family lived at Halton Place and they were keen on dancing. They often asked the band to play for events at their house and it became a favourite venue for the musicians.[40]

The number of musicians in the band depended on the number of people attending the dance and on special occasions they would add a cornet or clarinet player. If only two or three players were required for a dance, they would cycle to the hall. If there were four or more musicians needed, then a cab or wagonette was hired or they would travel by train.

Henry Wilson moved back to Settle in 1925 and it is from here that he set off one evening to a dance at Douk Ghyll. The event turned out to be far from comfortable. It was held in a barn and across the doors a cart cover prevented much, but by no means all, of the wind from entering. The barn was totally without heat and Henry Wilson and his two companions were obliged to keep their coats and mittens on throughout the evening. They were paid 10 shillings each for the dance, which started at 8 p.m. and finished at 4 a.m., with an interval for supper. Henry Wilson gave the violinist, a Burnley man, an extra 2 shillings from his own fee as his companion prepared to cycle all the way back to Burnley.

A sign would say 'Supper and Dance, 2 shillings and 6 pence'. This type of event was a regular attraction at Horton and Austwick. Henry regularly played at these events, often until 6 a.m., after which the workmen had just enough time to change into their working clothes. If he was required to play for another hour he would receive no extra money. 'I played until they couldn't dance any more.'

Once there was a 'two player' event at Downham School near Clitheroe. They went by train to Chatburn and then walked to the school. It was dark and they were not sure of the way. They made for a light in the window of a large house and asked directions. The two musicians took a short cut and both suddenly descended down a bank onto a roadway some four feet below. In the dance hall was a woman with a black eye who had evidently come to grief at the same place!

Snow was four feet deep one evening when Henry Wilson had to attend a dance at Malham and the owner of the waggonette, which had been hired, refused to turn out. Henry took a train to Bell Busk and walked to the hall from there. He arrived soaked to the skin and had to play in borrowed knee breeches. A cornet player joined him and they played until 4 a.m., after which Henry had to walk all the way back home.

Downham School is on the left; in the background is Pendle Hill. The school was also the venue for Mr Blackburn's dancing classes.

He often went on his bike to dances and would travel as far as Dent and Bursall. He said that he played for thirty-three years and never missed an engagement. He remembered an occasion when they played every night of the week in addition to their day jobs and he once presented a programme of seventeen old-time dances in one evening.

After the First World War

D ANCES did continue during the war years, though on a much reduced scale. Many band members were killed in the conflict and a considerable number of bands did not resume playing once the war was over. There were understandably fewer newspaper accounts of social activities between 1914 and 1918 and what dance events there were often took the form of a fund-raising enterprise in support of the war effort.

During the war, on 3 February 1917 for example, a *Preston Guardian* report described 'A successful Social and Dance, promoted by the residents

Unidentified band, photographed just after the First World War

of Higher Walton in aid of the local soldiers' comfort fund. A capable String Band, under the leadership of Mr William North, [augmented by] Matthew Worsley on the piano, provided the music for dancing.'

After the war, the better established bands did continue and there were many reports of Victory Balls and fund-raising events supporting the injured soldiers. However, there were new names appearing in the newspapers and it was also a chance for young bands and musicians to continue the tradition of playing for community dances.

During the 1920s, the influence of American Jazz on British entertainment meant that the composition and repertoire of dance bands began to alter. In turn, this led to the introduction of different instruments into the previously predictable line-ups. The music began to change. Added to that, American films were becoming popular and available to all, which also began to transform musical taste and dance fashion.

Matt. Worsley's Orchestra (Gregson Lane)

MATTHEW WORSLEY was born at Walton-le-Dale in 1885. In the 1901 census, he was described as a 'draper's junior'. The Worsley family were well known in the Gregson Lane and Bamber Bridge area and would visit their customers in the local villages with their draper's cart.

The first reference to Matthew Worsley's Band was in the *Preston Guardian* on 27 February 1909. 'The Annual Social Gathering took place at St Mary's Church, Brownedge. Mr Worsley's Gregson Lane Band provided the dance music.' Matthew was only 24 at the time.

The band must have been in existence during 1908 as the following report from 12 November 1910 indicates. 'Messrs Worsley's String Orchestra held their 3rd Annual Ball in the Drill Hall, Bamber Bridge. A large company attended.'

Matthew's chosen instrument is identified in this item dated 16 November: 'A Dance and Social under the auspices of Walton-le-Dale Football Club, took place in Walton-le-Dale Working Men's Club last Saturday evening. The pianist was Mr Worsley.'

4 January 1913: 'There was a large attendance at the Old School of Our Lady and St Patrick, Walton-le-Dale on Tuesday. Mr Worsley's Band played for dancing.'

Worsley's Orchestra, *c*.1913.[41] Matthew Worsley (second left with rolled sheet music), Jimmy Winter (trombone).

Worsley's Orchestra, *c*.1919.[42]

Matthew married Elizabeth Knight in 1912 and they continued to live in the village of Gregson Lane. The top photograph was taken around the same time, just before the outbreak of the First World War.

The following photograph was taken just after the First World War, when the band had resumed playing for dancing. It shows the difference in instrumentation with the addition of drum kit and saxophone instead of a flute. The influence of American style jazz changed the music, the sound and some of the dances.

The following advertisement appeared in the *Lancashire Daily Post* on 11 November 1920. Matthew continued to work from the family shop at 338

Gregson Lane and you can see from the advertisement that they are keen to play on any night of the week and this is probably with a busy day job as well.

The *Preston Guardian* reported on 3 February 1923 that 'The Annual Ball organised by the farmers of Bamber Bridge and District, was held in Brownedge St Mary's Hall. Dancing took place to the accompaniment of Matt Worsley's Band.'

DANCERS! DANCERS!—Requested to Book this Address:—WORSLEY'S ORCHESTRA, Gregson Lane; or C. HEAPS (Secretary), 34, Brook-street, Higher Walton. VACANT any Night except Saturdays.

advertisement 'Dancers! Dancers!

The band began to travel away from Bamber Bridge and Walton-le-Dale, the *Chorley Guardian* reporting on 24 January 1925 that 'A Fancy Dress Ball took place at the Parish Institute, Chorley. Worsley's (Brownedge) Orchestra provided the music for dancing.'

There must have been an augmented band for the following occasion. On 20 February 1926, the band played for the Leyland Motor's Annual Ball. It took place at the Thurston Road Canteen at the Leyland factory and the *Chorley Guardian* reported that '1,400 people attended the event'.

22 January 1927: 'The Fire Brigade Annual Ball took place at the Leyland Public Hall. Mr Worsley's Orchestra provided the music for dancing.'

22 January 1930: 'The Preston Farmers' Ball, held in the Public Hall, Preston, last night, was the twenty-fourth of the series and met with traditional success. A company of about 1,200 people were drawn from a radius of about 20 miles. Dancing proceeded to the music of Mr M. Worsley's Orchestra.'

In an article about Brindle Village Hall, the author remembered the band playing for a dance there. 'On special occasions a band lead by Matthew Worsley appeared. The dances were held from half-past seven until eleven, or midnight if it was some special event.'[43]

The orchestra went on to become the resident band at the Victoria and Station Hotel in Preston, which had its own ballroom and they were known there as simply the Victoria Hotel Orchestra. The band included Matt's two sons Harry and Frank on saxophones.

'Matt always said that the piano was an important instrument in the band and that it provided rhythm,' according to Matt's son. He also said that 'The band had different phases that reflected the dance fashions of the time. One of the big watershed moments for the band, as I recall my dad describing it, was the transition from Ragtime to Swing. They engaged a coach from Manchester to rehearse them in an American sound. One of the problems, repeated in other bands as I seem to recall the tale, was that many Ragtime dance bands contained brass band players. Ragtime and brass band playing used the same techniques, but Swing required different ones. Few brass band players made the transition successfully and Grandad eventually had to concede the position and replace the brass band lads amidst some ill feeling.'[44]

Matthew Worsley was also an organist at Our Lady and St Patrick's Roman Catholic church, Walton-le-Dale, for fifty years. He died in November 1962.

Leyland Motors Orchestral Band

THERE had been a number of string bands in the Leyland area, including the Leyland String Band (1889–1919) and E.H. Knowles' String Band (1892–1900).

Albert Parr's String Band (1909–22) provided music for a Leyland Motors Company social event. On 7 February 1914 an item recounts that 'The Annual Ball organised by Leyland Motors was held in the Public Hall, Leyland. Mr Parr's Full String Band supplied the music for dancing.'

There was also a Leyland Orchestral Band (1917–25). On 12 October 1918, an article mentions that 'A Dance and Whist Drive took place at Leyland Public Hall on Saturday evening. The event was for the Leyland branch of the Steam Engine Makers' Society. The music was supplied by the Leyland Orchestral Band.'

Leyland Motors employed a large number of people in the towns of Leyland and Chorley. The Leyland Motors Social and Athletic Club began life in 1919 and it had twenty-one different sections, including an orchestra and a celebrated brass band.

The above advertisement is from the *Lancashire Daily Post*, 29 August 1921. It tends to raise the intriguing question of whether the musical director, Tom Till, was employed directly by Leyland Motors or by the Motors' Social Club itself. The list of instruments required for the Motors' Orchestra is very similar to the line-up in the photograph of Tom Till's Band. Tom had previously been a cornet player in the Burnley Empire Theatre Orchestra.

The first reference to a Leyland Motors Orchestra is on 19 November 1921. 'Organised by the Leyland Motors Social and Athletic Club (Chorley Branch), a successful Whist Drive and Dance was held in the Town Hall,

WANTED, immediately, for Leyland Motors Orchestra (Chorley Branch) Performers for following instruments:—First and Second Violin. Violoncello. String Bass. Cornet. Clarionet. Trombone, Oboe, Bassoon. Horns, Drums, &c.; Ladies or Gents may apply.—Tom Till, Musical Director. Motor Works. Chorley.

Advertisement 'Wanted Immediately, for Leyland Motors Orchestra ...'

Photograph of Tom Till's Band.

Chorley, on Wednesday evening. Over 300 people took part in the dancing, the music being supplied by the works orchestra.'

A number of references record that the dances often took place in the vast canteens and workshops belonging to the company. In February 1922, for instance, 'The Annual Ball took place in the Work's Canteen. The Leyland Motors Social and Athletic Club's Orchestra played for dancing.' The orchestra played for every annual ball from 1922 until 1930, apart from 1926, when Matt. Worsley's Orchestra provided the music.

Also in 1922, on 11 November, an extract describes 'a large attendance at the Leyland Motors Canteen for a Ball organised by the Hockey section of the Social Club. Appropriate dance music was provided by the Leyland Motors Orchestral Band.'

From a report of 17 February 1923: 'The Leyland Motors Annual Ball was held in the Canteen last evening week. Over 500 people attended and the music was provided by the Leyland Motors Orchestral Band.'

Also in 1923, on 29 December: 'The Annual Carnival promoted by The Leyland Motors Social and Athletic Club was held last evening week in the Canteen at Thurston Road. The music was supplied by the Leyland Motors Orchestral Band under the conductorship of Mr T. Smalley.' Tom Smalley had also been bandmaster with Leyland Brass Band.[46]

A Leyland Motors Ball.[45]

The Chorley Weekly News of 22 January 1927 reported 'The Leyland Motors Annual Work's Ball was held a week ago in the firm's large hall off Hough Lane, Leyland. The Work's Orchestra (eleven players) under Mr A. Snape accompanied the dancing very efficiently.'

Arthur Snape also had his own band, mentioned in an article from 17 February 1923: 'The Leyland Morris Dancers' Annual Ball and Whist Drive took place in the Leyland Public Hall on Saturday evening. Mr Arthur Snape's Band provided the music for dancing.'

The photograph below was taken at the Annual Ball on 18 February 1928. 'The Leyland Motors Annual Ball took place in the Works Canteen. The Leyland Motors Symphonic Orchestra provided the music for dancing.'

Leyland Motors Orchestra, 1928.[47]

A GRAND BALL AND WHIST DRIVE
will be held in
THE WORKS CANTEEN THURSTAN ROAD,
LEYLAND. FRIDAY, Nov. 22nd, 1929.
Dancing from 7 30 p.m. to 2 a.m.
Whist Drive at 8 30 p.m.
Leyland Motors Orchestra.
12 Prizes for Whist.   Two Prizes for Lucky Spot
Dance.   Admission 2/-.
Late 'Buses to Preston, Chorley, and Earnshaw
Bridge.

advertisement (Grand Ball & Whist
Drive): *Lancashire Daily Post.*

Perhaps the term 'symphonic' was intended to elevate the orchestra's image. The remaining articles still refer to the band as an orchestra.

A report of the above dance appeared on 30 November 1929. 'In aid of the Preston Royal Infirmary Extension Fund, the Leyland Motors Social and Athletic Club held a Ball. There were 650 present and the music for dancing was supplied by the Leyland Motors Orchestra.'

Great Harwood Elite Orchestra

THERE are a number references to this young Great Harwood band in the *Burnley News*, all from the nearby village of Sabden.

The first article is from 12 December 1923: 'On Friday evening a Fancy Dress Ball was held under the auspices of Sabden Cricket, Football and Recreation Club in St Nicholas' School. There was a splendid attendance and the room was prettily decorated. The Elite Orchestra (Great Harwood) played for dancing and the MCs were Messrs C. and N. Moorhouse.'

From 2 December 1925: 'A Ball took place at St Mary's Roman Catholic School on Friday evening. The floor was specially prepared for dancing and the music was ably supplied by the Elite Orchestra from Great Harwood. There was a good attendance and a most enjoyable time was spent.'

3 March 1926: 'Last Saturday night a Social and Dance was held in the Sabden Council School under the auspices of the local branch of the National Union of Textile workers, Dyers and Finishers. Miss A. Westwell gave recitations, Miss E. Higham pianoforte solos, Mr John McDonald and Miss H. McDonald gave instrumental duets. The dance music was supplied by the Elite Orchestra.'

The Elite Orchestra, *c.1920*

Also in 1926, on 10 November: 'On Saturday a Dance under the auspices of the Sabden Conservative Association was held in St Nicholas' Church School. The Elite Orchestra provided the music and an enjoyable time was spent.'

Finally, from 23 March 1927: 'The Annual St Patrick's Ball was held in the Roman Catholic School last Friday night. The attendance was excellent and shamrock was very noticeable. The Elite Dance Orchestra of Great Harwood supplied the music and the MCs were Messrs J. Mahoney and H. Hill.'

Arcadian Dance Orchestra (Nelson)

THE photograph of the Arcadian Band shows an extremely youthful looking group of musicians, perhaps just after the First World War in the early 1920s.

There are a number of reports about the band in the *Burnley Express*. On

The Arcadian Dance Orchestra.

28 March 1926 an article recounts that 'On Tuesday evening the Burnley Branch of the Transport and General Workers' Union held their Annual Dinner at Greenwood's Café, Todmorden Road. Over seventy members and their friends sat down to a splendid repast. After dinner the Arcadian Orchestra played for dancing.'

In Barrowford on 24 June 1928: 'On Tuesday evening, in the Assembly Room, Church Street, Barrowford, the Co-operative Glee Union held a successful Social. The Arcadian Dance Band supplied the music for dancing.'

Finally, from 30 November 1929: 'Last Tuesday the Barden Bowling Club held a Whist Drive and Dance in the Duke Bar Assembly Rooms, Hebrew Road. After the refreshments, dancing took place to music supplied by the Arcadian Dance Band. Mr W.T. Green rendered songs which were greatly appreciated.'

IF YOU WANT YOUR DANCE to be a Great Success, don't hesitate to engage The Arcadians Dance Band for Dances, Parties, etc.—Terms, apply J. Snell, 11, Yorkshire-street (off Brunswick-street), Nelson.

Newspaper advertisement, *Burnley Express* 1928

Herbert Whittaker's Ladies' Orchestra (Lytham St Annes)

A NUMBER of orchestras played at the piers and pavilions along the Fylde coast in Lancashire. The Ashton Gardens Pavilion in St Annes, which opened in 1916, had Herbert Whittaker as the resident conductor with an all-female orchestra. The Pavilion had seating accommodation

Herbert Whittaker's Ladies'
Orchestra, 1917.

for 500 people but also had a maple floor that could be used for dances throughout the year.[48]

The Ladies' Orchestra was the resident attraction at the Ashton Gardens Pavilion. Most of the time they played in concerts which proved to be very popular. They did play for dances, however, as the following reports show.

In the *St Annes-on-the-Sea Express* of 25 July 1919 this item appeared: 'OUR PEACE CELEBRATION – The Pavilion was promptly arranged for dancing and with lifting music by the orchestra, the disciples of Terpsichore tripped it lightly until 11.45. Mr Whittaker and the ladies of the orchestra and all the others helped to make the evening a great success.' St Annes-on-the-Sea was the original name given to this nineteenth-century planned town, formally founded in 1875, now more often referred to as St Annes-on-Sea or simply St Annes. It lies to the south of Blackpool on the Fylde coast.

A *Preston Guardian* report of 6 November 1919 reads: 'At the Harris Free Library, Preston, last evening, the Mayor and Mayoress of Preston held a reception, which constituted a fitting ceremonial close to a period of office which will for long be distinguished in the annals of the ancient borough. Orchestral selections were rendered by Mr H. Whittaker's Ladies' Band. The Grammar School Choir provided a programme taking place in the Central Hall. Dancing was continued to 1 o'clock in the morning to the music of Mr Whittaker's Orchestra.'

The band continued to perform in the St Annes Ashton Gardens Pavilion. An article in 1921 refers to them as Miss Whittaker's Orchestra.

In the adjoining seaside resort of Lytham, similar bands played in the Floral Hall on the pier. In 1913, Miss Dorothea Vincent's Cremona Orchestra became a successful attraction and appeared every afternoon and evening. In the 1920s the Municipal Orchestra was a resident band in the Floral Hall until a fire destroyed the pier in 1928.

Lytham's residents and summer visitors could also enjoy the music in the Lowther Gardens and the Season Bands played between mid-June and mid-September.

There is a reference to a band playing in the Lowther Gardens on 5 August 1901: 'A successful Garden Party and Fete was held in the Lowther Gardens on behalf of the Cottage Hospital. The Lytham String Band was in attendance.'

In 1908 the newspaper reported that there was a move to replace the then string and reed band (who came from Preston Barracks) which had played for the previous three years in Lowther Gardens. The town council preferred a resident band for the holiday season, the argument being that 'the money paid would be spent in Lytham instead of on the railway and in Preston'.

The photograph below shows a string band at the official opening of the Lowther Park Bandstand on 17 July 1909, which cost £450 to construct.

The Lytham Season Band, 1909.

The *Lytham Times* report of 23 July 1909 declares that 'Mr Walter Bell is the bandmaster. His name is almost a household word in Lytham and he has got together an excellent combination of first-rate musicians, who will bye and bye make a band such as Lytham has never seen before.'

The Season Band continued after the First World War and a report in the *Lancashire Evening Post* of 3 October 1921 showed that they were very successful. 'The Lytham band season finished last night. Mr W.F. Holden, the chairman of the Council's Committee, announced that 38,520 people had been present at the concerts.'

Daniel Ellwood's Aeolian Orchestra (Fleetwood)

DANIEL ELLWOOD was born in Galgate near Lancaster in 1873. The family moved to live and work at Lane End's Farm in Pilling, Over Wyre, from where Daniel left to work in the fishing trade in Fleetwood, eventually becoming a fish merchant.

There is a local newspaper reference dated 22 February 1919, just after the First World War, which records Daniel playing music for dancing: 'A Fancy Dress Ball was held in the Pilling Church of England School. The music for dancing was supplied by Miss Louis Carter (piano), Mr Daniel Ellwood (violin) and Mr Whittaker (cornet).'

In the *Preston Guardian* of 22 December 1923 an event was covered in which Daniel is more than likely to have been involved. 'A Whist Tournament and Dance organised by the Fleetwood Blind Aid Society took place in the Co-operative Hall, Fleetwood, last evening week. The Aeolian Orchestra provided a capital programme of dance music.'

In 1924 Daniel lived at 52 Darbishire Road, Fleetwood, and was described as a Fish Merchants' Foreman. On 1 February of that year the *Fleetwood Chronicle* reported that 'A Dance in aid of funds for the St John Ambulance Brigade took place on Friday evening in the Co-operative Hall. Upwards of 300 people danced to the strains of the Aeolian Orchestra.'

20 December 1924: 'The Co-operative Hall, Fleetwood, was packed on Saturday night when a Whist Drive and Fancy Dress Carnival was held under the auspices of various guilds connected to the Fleetwood Co-operative Society. The music was supplied by the Aeolian Orchestra.'

Dan Ellwood is shown in the centre of the photograph with his violin

Dan Ellwood's Aeolian Orchestra at
Fleetwood's North Euston Hotel, 1927.

placed in front of the drum. The photograph of the band shows the change
in musical instrument types used by the late 1920s. The introduction of
the saxophone and the banjo, plus a different kind of drum kit, reflected
the changes in the style of music and the influence of American bands.

The reverse side of the band
photograph with details
of the orchestra.

DAN ELLWOOD and his AEOLIAN ORCHESTRA.

Pianist and Secretary   BILLY FINCH
to the Orchestra: of Wm. Finch & Son. Music Dealers.

During the Summer months Commencing April 27th. 1927
this popular orchestra will render the latest and most
successful dance numbers at

ONE SHILLING DANCES

in the Ballroom of the North Euston Hotel,

EVERY WEDNESDAY AT 7.30 TILL 11
and other dates as announced.

THE ORCHESTRA IS OPEN FOR ENGAGEMENTS.

93

PILLING   FARMERS'   BALL.

President: F. Whalley, Esq.

THE ANNUAL BALL AND WHIST DRIVE
will be held in the
COMRADES' HALL, PILLING,
WEDNESDAY, January 16th, 1935.
Through the generosity of our numerous patrons we are
again able to present a magnificent array of prizes.
WHIST at 7 p.m.   DANCING, 9 p.m.
TICKETS: GENT'S 2/6, LADIES' 2/-.
DAN ELLWOOD'S BAND (FLEETWOOD).

Advertisement in the *Lancashire Evening Post* for the 'Pilling Farmers' Ball', 1935.

The band continued into the 1930s. On 25 January 1935 the *Lancashire Evening Post* reported that 'The 17th Annual Ball arranged to benefit the Fleetwood Fishing Industry Benevolent Fund was attended by a large gathering in the Fleetwood Co-operative Hall, last night. Among the people present were many members of Fleetwood's trawler-owning firms. The music was provided by Mr Dan Ellwood's Orchestra.'

Finally, the band played in the Marine Hall, Fleetwood, on 28 November 1935 when the *Lancashire Evening Post* reported 'Following the Concert the public had their first opportunity to see the full range of coloured light when they attended a Long Night Dance. A non-stop programme of music was provided by the Dan Ellwood Orchestra.'

Withnell Fold String Band

THERE had been a number of references in the *Chorley Guardian* regarding small string bands in the Withnell area but, on 15 November 1919, the newspaper announced the formation of a new band. 'Under the auspices of the newly formed Withnell Fold String Band, a Dance was held in the Reading Room in the village. The proceeds were in aid of band funds.'

Another report from 9 October 1920 notifies its readership that 'There was a good attendance at a Dance at St. Paul's School, Withnell on Saturday evening. The Withnell Fold String Band, under the conductorship of Mr J. Hargreaves, provided the music.'

Withnell Fold Reading Rooms.

From a *Chorley Guardian* report of 3 December 1921: 'WORKPEOPLE'S SOIREE – The employees of the Calico Printer's Association Ltd. Brinscall Print Works, were well entertained to a Tea, Concert and Dance. It was held in St Paul's Schoolroom and music was supplied by the Withnell Fold String Band.'

18 February 1922: 'Under the auspices of the Withnell Fold String Band, a Dance was held in the Reading Room at Withnell Fold. The MCs were H. Roberts and T. Burton.' Howard Roberts and Tom Burton were members of Alban Yates' Band from Wheelton at this time.

Again, from 1922, on 11 November: 'A Dance was held in aid of funds for Withnell St. Paul's Football Club in the Schoolrooms on Saturday night. The Withnell Fold String Band provided the music for dancing.'

The *Chorley Weekly News* reported on 20 January 1923 and again on 10 January 1925 that the 'Withnell Farmers held a Ball at St Paul's School. The Withnell Fold String Band provided the music.'

This selection of references ends with a short extract highlighting the fact that, on New Year's Eve 1928, two dances took place in the village of Brindle. 'At the Institute was Alban Yates's Orchestra and at the School was the Withnell Fold String Band. Both dances were well attended.' Brindle is a very small village and to have two dances on the same night illustrates just how popular dancing was in the 1920s. The venues were on opposite sides of the road from each other on Water Street, Brindle.

Alban Yates' String Band (Wheelton) /
Arcadian Dance Band

ALBAN YATES was born in Town Lane, Whittle-le-Woods, in 1901 and came from a musical family of at least two previous generations.

His grandfather James Yates had been born in Whittle-le-Woods in 1843. He moved to live in Victoria Terrace, Wheelton and worked in Peter Todd's Victoria Cotton Mill in the village. In the mill he had the position of a supervisor known as an 'overlooker'. Having previously been a member of the Wheelton String Band, James went on to form his own string band along with his sons William and James jnr. On 4 February 1903, they appeared at the 3rd Annual Ball at Whittle Springs Hotel. 'Wednesday evening was the occasion of the Annual Ball at the Hotel. There was an attendance of over 100, a fair proportion being from Chorley. The music was supplied by Yates' Orchestra of Wheelton.'

The following reference relates to James' grandson, Alban Yates, and is taken from the *Chorley Guardian* of 1 November 1919, when Alban was only 18. 'The members of the Whittle-le-Woods Girls' Friendly Society party and friends sat down to an excellent hot-pot supper in the Church Clubroom. Alban Yates from Wheelton provided the music for dancing.'

Alban Yates and his band are mentioned on 12 November 1921, when the *Chorley Weekly News* reported that 'The Whittle-le-Woods Harriers held a Whist Drive and Dance at the Church Club on Saturday. There was a large attendance and Mr A. Yates's Band played for the dancing.'

A regular venue for many dances in the Wheelton area was recorded on 27 October 1923. 'In association with the Wheelton Cricket Club, a Whist and Fancy Dress Carnival was held at St Paul's School Room, Wheelton. Mr Alban Yates' String Band was in attendance.'

On 31 January 1925 the *Chorley Guardian* announced that 'A String Band under the leadership of Mr A. Yates, provided music at St Paul's Schoolroom, Wheelton'. The band continued to be in demand throughout the remainder of the 1920s at local dance venues.

During 1925 Alban's grandfather's band was still active, now run by James. On 14 February: 'The young farmers of Wheelton held a successful

Bamber Bridge C.C. advertisement in the *Lancashire Evening Post*, 8 November 1932

BAMBER BRIDGE C.C.—Dance, To-morrow. Yates' Elite Band. Presentation of Championship Medals (see advert.).

Alban Yates' String Band c.1925.
Tom Burton, Howard Roberts, Alban
Yates (piano) and Alan Marsden.

Whist Drive and Dance in St Paul's School, Wheelton. Mr J. Yates' Senior Band played for dancing.'

By the end of the decade, the term 'Orchestra' was used by the band and reflected the fashion of the times. For example, on 15 January 1927: 'The Withnell Branch of the National Farmers' Union held their Annual Ball in the St Paul's Schoolrooms last Saturday evening, when there were about 250 present. A. Yates' Orchestra played for dancing.'

18 October 1930: 'Alban Yates' Orchestra provided the dance music for the Heapey and Wheelton Tennis Club Dance which was held in the Council School in the village.'

The final reference to Alban Yates and his band was on 22 December 1934. 'The Withnell Fold branch of the Printers, Bookbinders and Papermakers held their 3rd Annual Dance at Whittle Springs Hotel on Saturday. The music was supplied by Yates' Elite Dance Band.'

Alban was a piano teacher and a familiar figure in the community as he cycled around the area giving piano lessons. The advertisement from the Brindle church magazine shows that he also repaired and tuned pianos. The official name for the band at this time was Yates' Elite Dance Orchestra, although it was still referred to locally as a 'string band'.

The address in the advertisement, 5 Victoria Terrace, Wheelton, was the house where his grandfather, James had lived. Alban became a widower and remarried in 1948 at St James church, Brindle, where he was the organist for over 40 years.

A. YATES,
Teacher of Pianoforte.
Pianos tuned and repaired.
YATES' ELITE DANCE ORCHESTRA.
FOR TERMS APPLY :
5 VICTORIA TERRACE,
WHEELTON, Nr. Chorley.

An advertisement for A. YATES, Teacher of Pianoforte, Wheelton.

In his role as church organist, Alban featured in an unusual article on 30 October 1933. 'One of the largest congregations ever seen at St Aidan's Church, Bamber Bridge attended a musical service in the style of 150 years ago, last night. There were over a thousand people present. The singing was accompanied by an orchestra of about a dozen instruments, some of them now obsolete, led by Mr. Yates, organist at Brindle Parish Church. The orchestra also gave several selections.'

The two fiddlers in the c.1925 photograph are Tom Burton and Howard Roberts. An article from 12 January 1924 refers to Howard Roberts' achievements. 'Violinist success – H. Roberts of Withnell Fold passed his intermediate grade. He is a pupil of J. Emmett of Wheelton.'

The author spoke to Joyce Coulborn, Howard Roberts' daughter, who still lives in Higher Wheelton. She remembers going to the dances at Withnell Fold and Brindle when her father played. He told her that he 'played the fiddle' for fellow POWs in the Second World War. He had continued to play in the band up to the 1940s and also had a spell playing in the Arcadian Dance Band. He worked at Withnell Fold Paper Mill and was very active in village life, including playing for the local cricket team.[49]

The cornet player is Alan Marsden. He worked at the Withnell Fold Paper Mill and had been a member of the Brinscall and Withnell Brass Bands plus, at a later stage, the Brindle Brass Band. Alan's son, Roy, was also a cornet player and drummer with various dance bands, including the Olympic Dance Band. He remembers clearly his father trekking over the fields from Higher Wheelton to Brindle to play for dances in the Brindle Institute.[50]

'The dances in the Withnell Fold Reading Room were very popular, especially if music was being provided by Alban Yates's Band from Wheelton, as they had a very good following, so it was always Full House on these occasions. The Reading Room was built in 1890 and upstairs was a large Concert Hall with a platform and a sprung dance floor.' [51]

The Brindle Institute became a very popular dance venue. 'The Club was open six nights of the week from seven till ten o'clock for members in return for their five shillings a year membership fee. All games were free and the evenings were well attended by young men employed on the local farms, as there were no other distractions as there are today. The Dance Hall was extremely popular, holding its weekly Saturday night dances, nearly always with a full house. Patrons came from all over the surrounding district. No doubt these occasions were the start of many a romance. The music was usually provided by Alban Yates' Elite Orchestra consisting of Alban Yates on the piano, Howard Roberts on the violin, Harry Jones on the drums and Alan Marsden on the cornet. All the musicians came from the Withnell Fold area, walking across the fields in summer and winter.' [52]

It was fairly common for a small village band, or trio, to consist of a piano, fiddle and cornet and there are numerous references from the area to support this supposition. The following four extracts actually concern the village of Rivington, north of Bolton, but the configuration of smaller groups of musicians was consistent throughout the county.

4 December 1897: 'A Bachelors' Party was held at the Rivington Church Schoolroom. Dancing commenced to the music of William Jolly (piano), Thomas Birchall (cornet) and Thomas Leeming (violin).' Thomas Birchall was also a cornet player with Rivington Brass Band. All three musicians lived on Chorley Road, Adlington.

There is a slight variation in the following account from 2 January 1897: 'On Thursday last, the Adlington Congregational Sunday Schools held a Social Gathering in the large Schoolroom. Dancing commenced at 7 p.m. and continued throughout the evening. The music was provided by Mr P. Shaw (piano), Mr W. Grime (violin) and Mr Crook (English concertina).'

From 6 January 1906: 'NEW YEAR'S GATHERING – The Annual Tea Party and Dance took place in the Chapel School, Rivington. Music was supplied by Messrs Harry Openshaw (violin), William Jolly (piano) and T. Miller (cornet).'

As late as 1930, the combination of instruments remained the same. From an item of January 28th that year: 'In association with Rivington Parish Church, the Church Tea Party and Parochial Gathering took place

Brindle Institute, 1923.

on Saturday last. Dancing then followed to the music supplied by Messrs Harry Openshaw (violin), Harry King (piano) and Len King (cornet).'

'In the Nineteen Twenties and well into the Thirties, people flocked to Brindle Parish Institute from surrounding areas, walking from Bamber Bridge and beyond. Dances and Whist Drives were held every Saturday night and the old building had a large hall that could easily accommodate 300 people. Dancing was to 'Yates' Elite Orchestra.'

'Alban Yates was on piano (he was also the church organist), Eddie Ambrose on drums, Howard Roberts on violin and Alan Marsden on cornet. The band was located on the stage, at the sides of which were two circular holes in the panelling, each fronted by discs of multi-coloured celluloid patches.'[53]

Arcadian Dance Band (Withnell)

THE ARCADIAN DANCE BAND was the natural successor to Alban Yates' Orchestra. Two of the original members had been in Alban's band and they continued to play at the same venues in the area.

The *Chorley Guardian* reported on a number of dances involving the Arcadian Dance Band. For example, on 1 January 1938: 'The Annual Catholic Ball took place at St Joseph's Church in Withnell. The Arcadian Band provided the music for dancing.'

During the war years, membership of the band changed as some were conscripted into active service. The band did, however, play for a fund-raising event, reported on 13 January 1940. 'The Brindle Ladies'

Lifeboat Guild held a Dance in the Parish Institute. The Arcadian Band provided the music for dancing.'

After the war the line-up of the band stabilised. The basics of the band were similar to Alban Yates' Band. Evan Pilkington on piano, Norman Pearson on cornet, Howard Roberts on violin (Howard had been a member of Alban's band). It also included Edith Dickinson on accordion and Sheila Rothwell on saxophone.

Evan Pilkington became the leader of the band. He was an accomplished pianist, having been taught by Alban Yates. Jack Pilkington, Evan's brother, remembers Alban cycling to the house to give piano lessons to his brother.

The band's regular practice venue was a room at Withnell Hospital, where Evan's father was the resident engineer. Norman Pearson worked at Withnell Gas Works and, if he was on night shift, the manager's wife would let them borrow her piano and they would practice in the Gas Work's Retort House.

Brindle Institute became a regular venue for the band along with other local halls, including Samlesbury and Hoghton. The Reform Club in Brinscall was also used along with schoolrooms in Wheelton and Withnell. When playing at Brindle, the Institute was heated by two pot-bellied stoves. The room was rather damp, which affected the felt hammers in the piano. The first job when the band arrived was to remove the back of the piano and put it near the stoves to dry out.

The largest piece of equipment, which had to be transported to each venue, was the drum kit. This was carried on a trailer towed behind a bicycle ridden by the 'roadie' Alan Jones from Withnell Fold. On one occasion, when cycling to Brindle, Alan was travelling at speed down Copthurst Lane when the brakes failed and he, his bike, the trailer and drum kit ended up in the ditch. Whenever the band played at Brindle, each musician would be paid eight shillings.

Dances included the Waltz, Valetta, Foxtrot, Barn Dance and the Gay Gordons, with music for a single dance usually consisting of a set of three tunes. Popular tunes of the day were used. 'Side by Side', for example, was used for the Barn Dance. The band had a copy of the piano music and everyone eventually got to know the tunes so well that they had no need to refer to any music. The band ceased playing in 1950.[54]

Related Bands

ALTHOUGH it was usual for string bands to provide music for dancing, there were other related musical bands that would perform a similar role. These included reed bands, concertina bands, brass bands and military bands. The range of dances and many of the dance venues were often the same as the ones used by string bands.

A full band was often far too large for the provision of dance music and it seems quite reasonable to expect that, depending on the size of the room, only a portion of the band would play.

The North Star Brass Band, Blackpool
– as a dance band 'combo', June 1925.

Brass Bands

THERE are numerous references to brass bands playing for dances and, with such a strong musical tradition in the county it is not surprising that brass instruments were used in some form of dance band combination.

At the Pilling Show on 2 September 1882, one reporter observed that 'during the day, the Pilling Brass Band was in attendance and discoursed dance music of every description, so keeping the 'country uns' in lively spirit'.

NEW POLKA FOR THE PRESTON GUILD. — THE BLACKPOOL PIER POLKA, beautifully illustrated with a view of the Pier, daily played by the Blackpool Subscription Band, and admired by all as the prettiest and best Polka of the day. To be had of Mr. RICHARDSON, corner of Lune-street, Preston; or of the composer, Mr. THOMAS GREEN, Netley House, Blackpool. Post free on receipt of twenty stamps.

From a piece about Higham which appeared on 7 July 1883, 'The teachers and scholars held their Annual Treat and Field Day. After being regaled with buns and coffee, games of cricket and football were indulged in until dusk. During the afternoon the Newchurch-in-Pendle Brass Band played for dancing.'

From Chorley on 2 January 1886: 'The 4th Annual Ball of the Gillibrand Rangers Football Club took place in the Town Hall on New Year's Eve and was attended by about 500 persons. Dancing commenced about 9 o'clock and was kept up until the small hours, to the strains of the Weldbank Brass Band under the leadership of Mr Thomas Jolly.'

In the Music Hall, Morecambe, 'a meeting took place of the Morecambe branch of the Fisherman's Lodge,' the *Lancaster Guardian* reported on 9 March 1889. 'After the meeting a Public Ball was held, there being about ninety couples present. The dance music was provided by the Bentham Brass Band and dancing was kept up with 'great spirit' until four o'clock on Thursday morning.'

From 8 June 1891: 'After the match between Colne and Littleborough on Saturday, a Gala was held on the Colne Cricket Field. The local Brass Band played for dancing and there was a large attendance.'

From an article of 20 August 1892 in the *Lancaster Guardian*: 'The 10th Annual Show of plants, flowers, fruits and vegetables under the auspices of the Caton and District Floral and Horticultural Society was held in a marquee in a field near Caton Railway Station. The Caton Brass Band was in attendance during the afternoon and evening and played selections of dance music.'

From Leyland on 21 January 1893: 'A Public Dance in connection with the Farrington North End Football Club took place on Saturday evening in the Assembly Room adjoining the Railway Hotel, Leyland. About 100 persons were present. The music was supplied by the Farrington Subscription Brass Band.'

Chipping Club Day took place on 13 May 1893. 'The usually quiet and secluded little village of Chipping was quite "en fete" on Thursday, the occasion being the celebration of the Annual Club Day.' After the meeting, 'the proceedings terminated and dancing to the strains of the Chipping Brass Band was subsequently indulged in.'

The coronation of Edward VII was celebrated at Samlesbury on 30 June 1902. 'The Field Day was held behind the Five Barred Gate Hotel and was attended by between 800 and 900 persons. Games were played during the afternoon and the Bamber Bridge Brass Band played for dancing.'

From an extract of 10 August 1905: 'The Cockerham Branch of the Primrose League held a Sports and Gala day. About 70 sat down to tea at the Old Manor Inn and later the Forton Brass Band played for dancing.'

In parts of Lancashire the local brass band would also play for morris dancing. In Bacup the Britannia Coco-nut Dancers still perform to their traditional music played by the Stacksteads Silver Band. In Leyland this

Leyland Prize Band playing for Leyland Morris Dancers in the May Festival procession, 1905.

style of brass band and morris dancing co-operation continued until recent times. For the Leyland Morris Men's 'Street Dance' the brass band played a set of jigs including Bonnie Dundee, Father O' Flynn, Hundred Pipers and Hexham Races.

There is an account of the Leyland May procession on 28 May 1908. 'The route was gaily decorated, lines of streamers crossing and re-crossing the road every score of yards. A marshal and a couple of amateur artillery men, mounted on gay chargers, led the way followed by the Leyland Prize Band and Morris Dancers, who performed as they went along.'

The *Burnley Express* reported on 31 October 1906 that, 'A public Tea was held at Trawden Primitive School on Saturday. The evening was spent in dancing. Four instrumentalists from the Trawden Brass Band played for dancing.'

1 August 1914: 'On Saturday last, the Withnell Industrial Co-operative Society held their Annual Procession and Field Day. Marching to the strains of the Brinscall and Withnell Band, the Morris Dancers attired in blue and white, who had been skilfully trained by Messrs J. Holland and R. Baker, went through their dances in a splendid manner.'

28 November 1917: 'On Saturday evening a Social and Dance, promoted by the operatives of the Worsthorne Manufacturing Company, took place in St John's School, the object being to raise funds to enable parcels to be sent to all the soldiers and sailors who have gone from the Mill. The Cliviger Prize Band played for dancing.'

ADMISSION.—Saturday: Sports 1/-, Dancing 6d.; Monday: Sports and Dancing 6d. Children under 14, Half-price.
CROSTON BRASS BAND
will be in attendance on Saturday and Monday, and will play for Dancing until 9 30 p.m.
James Dewhurst's Roundabouts and Shows will be on the Field.
For Entry Forms apply to the Secretary: JOHN T. NICKLIN, "Ivy Holme," Croston, Near Preston.

Croston Sports and Gala, 14 June 1930.

Rivington Brass Band

RIVINGTON BRASS BAND was formed about 1872. The band is still in existence today and is known as the Rivington and Adlington Brass Band.

Apparently, the band would often walk over the moors to play at Belmont church on Sunday morning and then have a few pints at the Black Dog Inn. Musicians in the back row of the 1895 photograph include Tom Birchall, Harry Birchall and in the front row, Jack Birchall.

There are a number of references in the *Chorley Guardian*, showing

Rivington Brass Band, c.1895.[55]

musicians playing with both the brass band and with small dance band combinations in the area.

From 11 January 1897: 'RIVINGTON SCHOLARS' FESTIVITIES – Dancing was held at Rivington Elementary School. The music was provided by M. Makinson (piano), D. Makinson (violin) and T. Birchall (cornet).'

On 2 November 1901 the *Chorley Guardian* reported that Mr S. Leeming was the bandmaster of the Rivington Brass Band. A week earlier he had been playing in Adlington as the leader of his own string band. On 6 December 1902, 'The Annual Social in connection with the Cycling Club was held at the Elephant and Castle Hotel, Adlington. Dance music was supplied by S. Leeming's String Band.'

2 January 1897: 'The Adlington Football Club held a Dance at the National School. The music for dancing was provided by Messrs W. Jolly (piano), J. Hough (cornet) and S. Leeming (violin).'

There are a number of accounts of Rivington Brass Band playing for dancing. On 2 November 1907: 'In connection with The Adlington and Heath Charnock St John Ambulance Brigade, their 8th Annual Ball was held on Saturday evening. The music for dancing was provided by the Rivington Brass Band.'

After the First World War, on 4 January 1919, the *Chorley Guardian* reported that 'A successful Victory Ball was held in the Parish Church Schoolrooms on New Year's Eve. Music was supplied by the Rivington Band.'

Finally, on 9 February 1924, this brief account was published: 'On Saturday last, a Dance was held in Adlington St Paul's School. The

Rivington Band was in attendance and a good programme of dances was enjoyed, including the Polka and the Barn Dance.'

East Lancashire Concertina Bands

CONCERTINA BANDS first appeared in the early 1880s and consisted of various sizes of English concertina (a fully chromatic instrument with the range of a violin) and percussion. They played a similar repertoire of tunes to the brass bands and often appeared in processions and concerts. The concertina bands also played for dancing as the next few references show.

The band in the photograph is mentioned in the 12 August 1882 edition of the *Blackburn Standard*: '700 scholars assembled at the School at two o'clock and were arranged in processional order, headed by the Livesey Brass Band, whilst the Accrington and Church Concertina Band brought up the rear. The concertina band, being a novelty, attracted much attention.'

Accrington and Church Concertina Band, c.1882.[56]

Also in the *Blackburn Standard* of 29 May 1886 was this account: 'An Annual Gathering of the members of the Burnley branch of the Irish National Land League was held on Saturday night. Tea was served at the rooms of the league in Chaffer Yard, there being about 270 present. An adjournment was made afterwards to St James' Hall, where the number of about 300 indulged in dancing. The music was supplied by St Mary's Brass and Concertina Bands. Songs were also given and the evening was very pleasantly spent by all.'

'Feniscowles Hall – A Concertina Band', an advertisement in the *Lancashire Evening Post*, 26 May 1887.

FENISCOWLES HALL.—A Concertina BAND
will play for DANCING on the Green on WHIT-MONDAY,
TUESDAY, and WEDNESDAY AFTERNOONS.—B. CARLISLE, Prop.

On 3 April 1888, the *Blackburn Standard* reported: 'FOOTBALL CLUB SOIREE – On Saturday evening a very enjoyable soiree was held in the Burnley Mechanics' Institute, promoted by the Burnley Union Star Football Club. There were about 300 present. The music for dancing was supplied by the Catholic Concertina Band and songs were given at various intervals.'

The popular Keighley Concertina band from Yorkshire, were booked to play in Colne in November 1888. The *Burnley News* commented on 7 November that 'In the Assembly Room of Colne Cloth Hall, a Ball took place on Saturday night and the affair was very largely patronised. The Keighley Concertina Band, numbering over forty performers, played selections of dance music. Mr H. Haigh was the band leader and Mr J. Ashworth officiated as Master of Ceremonies.'

A week later, on the 14th, the paper also ran a similar story. 'WORKPEOPLE'S GATHERING – About 250 of the hands at Great Holme Shed held a Social Party in the Cloth Hall on Monday night to celebrate the marriage of two of their number. The Primet Bridge Concertina Band played for dancing after tea had been partaken of, Mr Poole conducting.'

The Queen's Hall, Nelson, proved to be a popular venue for dances. On 16 April 1890, another item appeared. 'Ball at Queen's Hall – The

'Dancing Every Saturday Evening', an advertisement in the *Burnley Express*, 10 February 1892.

**DANCING EVERY SATURDAY EVENING
AT QUEEN'S HALL, NELSON.
BURNLEY CATHOLIC CONCERTINA
BAND, FEBRUARY 13th, 1892.
Admission 6d. each.**

new Hall, recently opened by Mr Hargreaves, has already become very popular and this week another Ball was given where about 200 couples were present. Music was supplied by the Nelson Concertina Band and Bradley's String Band.'

The following article in the *Burnley Express* is from the village of Trawden, near Colne, and published on 10 February 1894. 'The operatives of J. & J. Hopkinson, together with their employers, in all numbering about 100, partook of a knife and fork Tea on Saturday evening in the National Schoolroom. The local concertina band supplied the dance music and a very pleasant evening was spent.'

On 23 November 1907, the *Burnley Express* reported: 'On Saturday the young men attending St Mary's School, Newchurch-in-Pendle gave a Potato Pie and Social. At the Social a concertina band played for dancing, the proceeds were in aid of a new piano for the school.'

In the *Burnley News*, 8 April 1922: 'A Concert was given by the Byerden House English Concertina Band which was greatly appreciated by the patients and staff. After the interval the band went through a programme of dance music.' The band was based at the Byerden House Socialist Club on Colne Road, Burnley.

East Lancashire Reed Bands

THE *Blackburn Standard* published various reports of reed bands in the east of the county, bands comprising flutes, piccolos and clarinets plus percussion.

Clitheroe Brass and Reed Band

THE first mention of the Clitheroe Brass and Reed Band was on 28 July 1877. 'About midway through the procession came the Clitheroe Catholic Brass and Reed Band, under the leadership of Mr M. Duckett.'

Although the band's main purpose was to provide music for processions, it is evident that they also played for dancing, as this article of 23 August 1879 shows: 'On Saturday afternoon last, members of the Clitheroe Liberal

Members of the Clitheroe
Catholic Reed Band.[57]

Club visited Read Hall, near Whalley. As the members arrived at the hall, the Clitheroe Catholic Band played a selection of music on the field in front of the hall. The band played for dancing in a field adjoining the hall.'

29 October 1881: 'The Ball held annually in connection with St Michael and St George's Catholic Church on the night of the Fair, took place on Saturday last in the Public Hall. The music was furnished by the Catholic Band, with Matthew Duckett as conductor.'

Clitheroe Public Hall was the venue mentioned in an item published on 19 August 1882. 'During the afternoon the Catholic Band, with Mr Matthew Duckett as leader, discoursed a varied selection of music to the pleasure of the auditors. In the evening the same band played for dancing, when a large company was assembled.'

Accrington Primrose Reed Band

ACCORDING to an article in the *Blackburn Standard* of 31 July 1886, one of the main reasons for the formation of the Accrington Primrose Reed Band was to play 'patriotic music'. Although they appeared in processions and events at the Conservative Club, they regularly play for dances too. George Thornton, Professor of Music in the town, was entrusted with the task of creating a band that would always be at the disposal of the Conservative Association and of the Primrose League.

From a story published on 23 July 1887 comes this description: 'On Saturday afternoon the Primrose League visited Moreton Hall for a picnic. About 200 made the journey by waggonette, starting from the Conservative Club. They were accompanied by the Accrington Reed Band, which played selections. On arriving at the hall, dancing was indulged in to the strains of the Reed Band.'

The Accrington Reed Band.[58]

The band even promoted events for themselves. This account from 7 December 1889 illustrates this regular practice. 'The Annual Ball in connection with the Accrington Primrose Reed Band took place at the Accrington Town Hall on Wednesday night. There was a large attendance and the Ball was a success.'

On 31 January 1891 the last reference to the band playing for dancing came in this report: 'An enjoyable Ball took place in the new Conservative Club, Accrington. The Ballroom was tastefully decorated by Mr Hudson of Burnley and was brilliantly lighted by electric light provided by Mr Simpson of Hapton. The Accrington Reed Band supplied the music.'

Bank Hall Reed Band

BANK HALL was a large residence near to the centre of Burnley. The Bank Hall Reed Band was funded by local benefactor Sir John Hardy Thursby. He was Colonel of the 5th Lancashire Militia and his battalion had training facilities at Bank Hall Meadow, which was part of the Thursby estate.

Bank Hall Reed Band.

In the *Burnley Express* of 11 June 1897 was this reference: 'On Monday afternoon the field was set apart for the enjoyment of the scholars. The Bank Hall Reed Band was in attendance and played selections of music and accompaniments to dancing.'

On 5 March 1913 the *Burnley News* reported: 'In connection with the Bank Hall Reed Band, a dance was held in the Mechanics' Institute on Saturday evening and there were a large number of guests.'

The Mechanics' Institute was a popular venue for the band. They played for another dance on 24 February 1915 in aid of funds for the Bank Hall Hospital. The following advertisement shows that the band was still providing dance music in the 1920s.

MECHANICS' INSTITUTE,
SATURDAY, APRIL 3rd,
GRAND EASTER DANCE,
Promoted by the BANK HALL REED BAND.
7 to 11 p.m. M.C.: J Bridge. Latest Music.
— 1/6 —

Advertisement for a 'Grand Easter Dance at the Mechanics' Institute, 3 April 1920.

St Joseph's Harmonica Band (Withnell)

S LIGHTLY out of the timeframe of this publication's title were the harmonica bands of the 1930s. The bands featured in American films and became popular in this country as the instruments were relatively affordable. St Joseph's Band members played different size harmonicas and they included a drum kit in their line-up, played by Jimmy Murphy. They practised in the church schoolrooms on Bury Lane, Withnell.

Jack Corrigan was the leader and instigator of the band. They played at various places in the locality, but Withnell St Joseph's Schoolrooms, the Reform Club on Railway Road, Brinscall and the Canteen in Hargreaves' Silk Mill were their most common venues.

The *Chorley Guardian* reported a number of events when the band played for dancing. On 23 January 1937: 'A dance was held at St Joseph's School, Withnell, on Thursday last, when Mr H. Trencher was the MC. The music was supplied by the St Joseph's Harmonica Band.' Again, on 13 February 1937: 'A Shrovetide Dance was held at St Joseph's School, Withnell. The Church Harmonica Band provided the music.'

An extract from 20 October 1938 informed that 'The Dramatic Society of St Joseph's R.C. Church, Withnell, held a successful Social in the School on Tuesday night. About 60 members danced to the music of the church's own band.' Also, a 17 December 1938 report related that 'A successful Dance and Social was held in St Joseph's R.C. School, Withnell, on

St Joseph's Harmonica Band, *c.*1939.[61]

Wednesday. St Joseph's Dance Band, led by Mr J. Murphy provided music for the dances.'

The band reformed briefly after the Second World War and continued to play for local dances in and around Withnell and Brinscall. Lucy Harwood remembered travelling with her brother to see them play at St. Chad's Club in Whittle-le-Woods. Their dance repertoire was not dissimilar to other dance bands in the area.

Cinema / Dance Orchestras / Fred Horsfield's Orchestra (Coppull)

WITH the advent of cinematography, it was not unusual for dance bands to earn extra income by playing at the local cinemas to provide background music for silent films.

The Albert Hall Cinema, situated on Duckworth Street, Darwen opened in 1913. Darwen's first cinema was originally intended to be a factory, but the builder had gone bankrupt, resulting in its conversion into a cinema. The 'best' seats, forms covered with velvet, cost 6*d.*, back seats and wooden benches cost 3*d.* The Albert Hall presented 'turns' as well as films.

The owner of the cinema was Harry Holden. He went straight from school into his father's photography business. He had a studio in Darwen,

The Albert Hall Cinema
Orchestra, Darwen.

where his wife Ellen was a colourist. He worked in his photographic studio during the day and was cinema manager in the evenings.

Harry Holden was also a professional flautist, doing freelance performances and playing in the Blackburn Philharmonic. He later moved to Southport, where he played the flute at Boots café and in the Pier Orchestra. Harry Holden died on 8 August 1928.[59]

SITUATION Wanted, Cornet Player, Cinema or
Theatre Orchestra.—Box W, Sandiford's, Chorley.

'Situation Wanted, Cornet Player' for a
cinema or theatre orchestra, *Lancashire
Evening Post*, 18 August 1921.

Initially some silent films were accompanied by individual musicians or, in the case of the Albert Hall Cinema, a small orchestra. Later Cinema Organs were specially designed to mimic traditional orchestral instruments and were installed in many cinemas. When 'talkies' came along in 1929, the orchestras were disbanded.

Fred Horsfield's Orchestra (Coppull)

ONE orchestra that did provide that dual role of being a cinema orchestra and a dance band was Fred Horsfield's Orchestra from the village of Coppull near Chorley. Fred Horsfield was born in 1902. He came from a family of colliery workers and lived at Jolly Tar Lane in Coppull.

He originally played in a small dance band connected to St Wifred's

Church in nearby Standish. The band consisted of Fred on violin, Sidney Howard on cello and Jane Critchley on piano. There was also a clarinettist.

Jane was from a local family in Standish. By the age of 14 she had lost both her parents and was brought up by her elder brother. She worked in the local cotton mill and did extra work cleaning the steps of houses so that she could fund her piano examinations. She moved to live in Chorley in 1928 and became a piano teacher. She was able to play for dancing as a solo pianist and became involved with St Peter's church in Chorley.

Fred and his band played at the Picture Palace Cinema on Regent Street in Coppull at the beginning of the 1920s. The band would have to produce music to accompany the silent films. The music would have to be not only spontaneous but convincingly appropriate to the action taking place on the screen.

Most of his playing of dance music took place around the Coppull district and the following article is typical of the *Chorley Guardian*'s references to the band. On 9 February 1929 the paper published this item: 'The Coppull Farmers' Annual Ball took place at Chapel Lane School, Coppull on Saturday last. There was a record attendance for the event and Mr Horsfield's Orchestra played for dancing.'

Fred was a well-known figure in the Coppull area, not only as a musician but as an insurance agent for the Prudential Insurance Company. He would cycle around the district collecting money each week.

He continued playing in a trio (fiddle, piano and drums) up to 1952 and would often play in the Coppull Parish Church Schoolrooms. Fred would 'saw away' at the fiddle and, if he got fed up playing, would suddenly put down the violin and start singing instead. A number of his dance tunes had been adapted from popular songs of the day.[60]

Church String Bands in Chorley

T HE church was at the heart of social life for many people and a number of churches had their own string bands to accompany choral singing in its various forms. In some cases, the bands would also provide music for social dancing, with churches often promoting their own dances for fund-raising functions and social events.

The *Chorley Guardian* printed a number of accounts of string bands from various churches in the town. On 27 January 1894, for example, this information appeared within an item: 'The St Joseph's String Band, conducted by Herr Pressler, discoursed popular music at intervals.'

The first account of a church band actually playing for dancing was on 30 November 1901. 'A Social Gathering took place at St Peter's Social Club on Wednesday evening, when about 100 persons were present. Dancing then took place to the accompaniment of St Peter's String Band.'

Just before the new Parish Church Institute was built on Park Road, Chorley, on behalf of St Laurence's Church, the newspaper reported a fund-raising effort in support of the project. On 4 January 1902, the article declared that 'A Social in aid of the Parish Church Institute was held in the Parker Street School on New Year's Day. St Laurence's String Band played for dancing.'

12 January 1907: 'The 23rd Annual Ball of the Chorley Catholic Club took place at the Town Hall. Over 600 persons were present, the music was provided by St Mary's String Band.'

Long after St Laurence's Church Institute had been built their dance orchestra was still active, continuing well into the 1920s. On 7 February 1925 an account declared 'At the Parish Church Institute, Chorley, a very

St George's Church Orchestra,
Chorley, c.1925.

successful Dance was held last Saturday, (at which) about 130 persons were present. The Church Institute Band, conducted by Mr A. Williams, provided an excellent programme of dance music.'

St Mary's Catholic Church Institute was also a thriving Social Club with its own busy orchestra. A piece from 27 February 1927 mentions that, 'The usual weekly Dance was held on Saturday evening for which the St Mary's Orchestra supplied the music. The same instrumentalists played for a dancing class on Monday evening at the church.' The Church Orchestra became known as the Pleasant Players Orchestra after the location of the Church at Mount Pleasant. This in turn changed its name to the popular Bert Barker Band.

St Gregory's Roman Catholic Church also had an orchestra. On 25 January 1928, 'There was a dance on Saturday evening at St Gregory's Institute, Weldbank, in Chorley. The Institute Orchestra, comprising J.S. Turner (piano), G. Moore and W. Rainford (violins), L. Porter (cello), H. Baron (banjo) and J. Waring (drums), provided the music for dancing.'

St Peter's Institute Band played for a fund-raising event which was reported on 6 December 1930 by the *Chorley Weekly News*: 'St Peter's Football Club held a Dance in aid of team funds. The band comprised of Messrs W. Renton (piano) A. Brook (violin) and J. Cottam (drums).'

Advertisement for a dance at St Mary's Hall to be held in December 1928.

ST. MARY'S HALL.
TO-NIGHT.   TO-NIGHT.
SATURDAY, 15th December, 1928.
USUAL DANCE, 7-0 to 11. p.m.
Four Prizes for Spot Dances.
Music by "Pleasant Players Orchestra.
Admission 1s. 3d inclusive.

Dance Venues

APART from the large Assembly Rooms in the towns and cities, dancing took place in any available space or room, including schoolrooms, reading rooms, public houses, inns, church rooms and workplaces, including cotton mills.

The *Preston Guardian* printed an article on 7 January 1860 concerning Wheelton Cotton Mill, near Chorley: 'On Saturday last, there was a pleasing scene in the township of Wheelton, such as has never been witnessed there before. Messrs W. and P. Todd, having completed a new part of their extensive works, gave their workpeople a most hospitable and liberal treat in a large room of their new building. After the toasts, the tables were removed and the remainder of the evening was spent by many of the company in a pleasant Social Dance. An excellent band of musicians were in attendance, who added much to the entertainment of the evening by playing many lively airs.'

Dance at Hartford Mill, Oldham, given by Mr Platt to 500 of his workpeople. An illustration from the *London Illustrated News*, 16 January 1864.

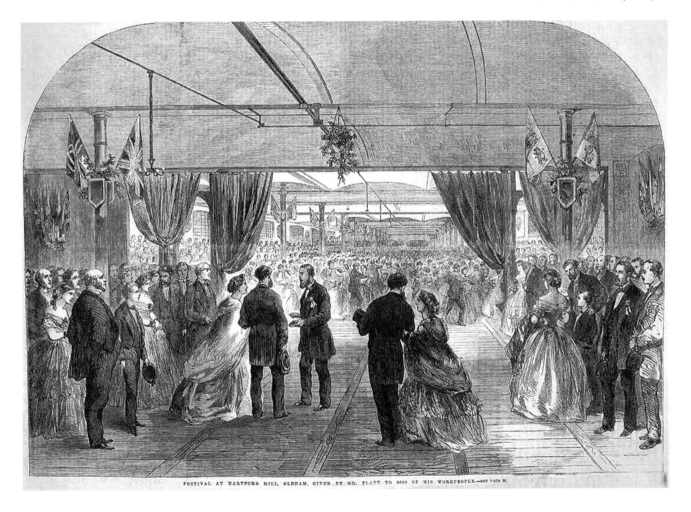

FESTIVAL AT HARTFORD MILL, OLDHAM, GIVEN BY MR. PLATT TO 5000 OF HIS WORKPEOPLE.—SEE PAGE 82.

From Darwen on 20 February 1864: 'On Saturday the hands employed at Industry Mill, under the firm of Aspden, Walmsley & Cooper, had tea in one of the rooms of the new premises of the mill. Mr. Richard Hargreaves' Quadrille Band was present and the company danced with great glee until a late hour.'

At the end of the nineteenth century many new Co-operative stores included a large dance hall on the first floor. The Longridge Co-operative Hall often had up to 500 people at the dances held there.

Long Nights

E VENTS known as 'Long Nights' became popular in Lancashire. As well as the dancing, the evening would contain features such as songs, recitations, monologues and clog and step dancing. As the name suggests, these gatherings would often last well into the early hours of the morning.

'Mr Collinson's Long Night': An advertisement from the *Preston Guardian*, 26 December 1891, promoting a Long Night event with John Collinson's String Band.

MR. COLLINSON'S LONG NIGHT on NEW YEAR'S EVE. Gentlemen, 1s 6d ; Ladies, 1s.—4, St. James's-road, Moor Park.

Tommy Ainsworth was a music teacher in the village of Withnell and is pictured with some of his pupils. He also had his own dance band. Frances Bolton is pictured on the extreme left of the photograph, holding a mandolin.[62]

The term Long Night was used in this village event reported in the *Preston Guardian* of 30 January 1904: 'DOLPHINHOLME VILLAGE READING ROOM – LONG NIGHT DANCE – This annual function, which is looked forward to with great interest, was held in the Reading Room on Thursday last week. The night was all that could be desired – no small matter for the success of a Country Dance.'

Frances Bolton appears in the following article when, in 1906, the Yates family of Wheelton promoted three events during the year, all reported in the *Chorley Guardian*. 'Yates' 3rd Social Dance was held in the Wheelton Council Schoolrooms. Mr W. Standish was the MC for the concert. Mr E. Yates (banjo soloist), Miss F. Bolton (mandolinist) and Mr F. Chadwick (accompanist) played a selection of music. Yates's String Band, ably assisted by Mr J. Heaton (Chorley) and Master G. Robinson (Wheelton), rendered their dance music in an excellent manner.'

From 14 December 1912: The Long Night organised by the Garstang Football Club was held in the Liberal Club on Thursday evening. A most enjoyable evening was spent and music for dancing was supplied by Mr H. Towers.'

7 February 1914: 'On Wednesday a Tea and Social was held in the Co-operative Hall, Haslingden. There was a piccolo solo by Mr W. Heap and a selection by the Concertina Band under the conductorship of Mr Brown. Mr Harry Heap's String Band played for dancing.'

5 November 1921: 'A Long Night Dance was held on Friday. The proceeds were in aid of the Galgate Orchestral Band by whom the music was provided.'

WALTON FOOTBALL CLUB.—DANCE (Long Night). WORKING MEN'S INSTITUTE, MONDAY, Dec. 26th. Admission 1/-. 7 30 p.m.

Walton Football Club, from the *Lancashire Daily Post*, 3 December 1921.

As late as 21 March 1934, the *Burnley Express* reported: 'FOR CLOG FUND – In aid of their Clog and Shoe Fund, the Education Committee of the Weavers' Association held a Long Night Dance and Supper in the Barnoldswick Co-operative Hall last Friday.'

James Clegg's Long Nights

J AMES CLEGG was born in Blackburn in 1860 and lived most of his life in Longridge. He became renowned in the town and surrounding villages for his Lancashire dialect recitations. He also organised large social events known as Long Nights which became very popular.

Many accounts of James Clegg's social organising centre on the Co-operative Hall, Longridge, the first one here being from 3 December 1887: 'The 5th Annual Ball in connection with St Lawrence's (Longridge) Brass Band was held in the Co-operative Hall, Longridge. The band, under the able conductorship of Mr T. Sallers discoursed several selections in a manner showing steady improvement. There was a duet, The Huntsmen's Chorus, played on the violin and piano by Mr E. Crook and Mr William Helm. Mr James Clegg gave a Lancashire recitation "Uncle Dick's Advice to Single Women". The usual votes of thanks closed the Concert and then the Ball followed.'

James Clegg obviously organised many concerts and social events, another of which is mentioned in the next reference, from 15 October 1892. 'The first Concert of the season took place in the Co-operative Hall on Saturday evening. It took the form of a Comic Carnival and had been arranged by Mr James Clegg.'

The *Preston Guardian* also carried a number of references concerning James Clegg. On 28 January 1899 it contained the following item: 'MR JAMES CLEGG'S SOCIAL – The popular Lancashire reciter Mr James Clegg of Longridge held his 2nd Annual Social in the Co-operative Hall on Saturday. The affair was well attended. A capital programme of songs, recitations etc. was gone through in a very creditable manner. Mr James Clegg gave several Lancashire recitations. Turners Orchestral Band supplied an excellent programme of dance music.'

James Clegg was also in demand in the surrounding villages. An extract from 9 January 1904 describes a local event: 'On New Year's Eve, the quaint village of Chipping held a most successful Sale of Work and a Dance. It was held in the New Brabbins School in Chipping. Jas. Clegg of Longridge gave several comic recitations and the Chipping String Band performed the dance music.'

He also appeared in the village of Thornley. 14 October 1905: 'There was a Social at Thornley School in aid of school funds. Dancing was indulged in to music supplied by Mr Alston's Band and during the evening Mr Clegg of Longridge gave some enjoyable recitals of Lancashire dialect.'

Reported on 27 November 1915 was the news that 'Clegg's Long Night with the Longridge Orchestral Band on Saturday night raised the sum of £6 7s. 6d. A total of 18,000 cigarettes, 200 quarter lbs of tobacco and 600 chocolate bars had been bought from R. Cross for dispatch to the troops.'

Clegg's Long Night, *Lancashire Daily Post*, 1920.

CLEGG'S LONG NIGHT. CO-OPERATIVE HALL, LONGRIDGE, SATURDAY, August 28th. Dancing from 7 until 11. 1/- each. Late train to Preston 11 10 p.m.

Clegg's Long Nights became increasingly popular and people would travel from quite a distance to them, as the above advertisement suggests. After the war The Longridge Orchestral Band played for the majority of events in the Longridge Co-operative Hall.

The following article appeared on 5 January 1935: 'On New Year's Day Mr and Mrs James Clegg, 76 Mersey Street, Longridge, celebrated their Golden Wedding. They were married at Longridge Parish Church by the Rev. F.A. Cave-Brown-Cave on January 1st 1885. Mr Clegg started work in a cotton mill at 8 years of age and retired at the age of 74, being employed in the mill the whole of that time, with the exception of four years which he spent in a stone quarry. For 47 years he was employed at Messrs Hayhurst & Marsden's Mill, Longridge, and was a collector for the Longridge Weavers Association for 44 years. During the War [1914–18] he organised what were known as Clegg's Long Nights and raised nearly £500 for the soldiers.'

References and Acknowledgements

Lancashire Map

With thanks to David Nelson.

Music and Dance

1 Lancashire Record Office, ref. DDX978/1/18/6.
2 'The Winders of Wyresdale' by Andy Hornby.

Church Bands

3 'The Musicians of Rossendale' by Jean Seymour — West Gallery Music Association.
4 Instruments and MSS on display in the Whittaker Museum, Rawtenstall.
5 The James Nuttall manuscript and the Winder family manuscript are available on the Village Music Project website www.village-music-project.org.uk
6 'A brief history of Holy Trinity Parish Church' by G.C. Mille — Blackburn Times Press 1973.

Crosse Hall Band

7. 'A history of Chorley' by Jim Heyes — Lancashire County Books 1994.

Robert Gudgeon's Band

8 Tom Holgate was interviewed on 26 March 1960, when he was 87, by Tom Flett and Julian Pilling — notes courtesy of Lindsay Smith (daughter of Tom Flett).
9 'Clitheroe in the Coaching and Railway Days' by Stephen Clarke — Landy Publishing 1989.

J.W. Collinson's String Band

10 Photograph — courtesy of the Harris Library, Preston.

Bateson's Band

11 'Fenty's Album' by Irvine Hunt — Pinewoods Publications 1975.
12 Photograph — courtesy of Andy Hornby.

Higher Walton String Band

13 Photograph — courtesy of Anne Bradley, Higher Walton.
14 'The life of Kathleen Ferrier' by Winifred Farrier — Hamish Hamilton 1956
15 'The story of handbell ringing in Higher Walton' by Enid Catterall — 2007.

James Winder's Band + William Brockbank's Band

16 Information from Bill Winder, the grandson of James Winder, Dolphinholme in August 2010.
17 Music from the manuscripts and background information 'The Winders of Wyresdale' by Andy Hornby.
18 'The Winder Family' — Lindsay Smith and Chris Pollington — Information is taken from Tom Flett (Lindsay's father) notes when he visited Wyresdale in 1960. He interviewed nine people in relation to social and step dancing in the area.
19 'Galgate in Focus' by Ruth Roskell — Landy Publishing 2007

Blackpool Central Pier Orchestra

20 Blackpool Council.
21 'Lancashire's Seaside Piers' by Martin Easedown — Wharncliffe Books.

Longridge Orchestral Band

22 Photograph – courtesy of Longridge Heritage Centre.

23 Information about the photograph is from Jim McDowell. His father joined the Longridge Orchestral Band as a clarinet player shortly after the photograph was taken. Jim played clarinet and fiddle in the St. Wilfred's Orchestra 1934 – 1939 and had his own dance band after the Second World War.

24 'Popular Entertainment in the Longridge Area in the nineteenth and early twentieth centuries', copy in the Harris Library, Preston – Peter Vickers.

Whittingham Asylum Band

25 'Longridge: the way we were', containing an article by Peter Vickers in a compilation by the Longridge and District Local History Society – Hudson History 1999.

26 'Times past in Goosnargh' by Angela Dewhurst – Countryside Publications 1985.

Chipping String Band / Henpecked Club

27 Photograph – courtesy of Longridge Heritage Centre.

Gregson's String Band

28 Photograph – courtesy of St Annes Library – thanks to Andrew Walmsley and Martin Ramsbottom for their help.

Samuel Hobson's Band

29 Photograph and information – courtesy of Alan and Jean Seymour.

Stanhill String Band

30 'Old Homesteads of Accrington and District' by Richard Ainsworth – Wardleworth, Accrington 1928.

31 Photograph – courtesy of Accrington Library, thanks to John Simpson for his help.

32 Hall – Genealogy Website.

33 Photograph – Accrington Web.

Huncoat String Band

34 Photograph – Accrington Web.

Byer's Orchestra

35 Photograph – courtesy of Wigan Archives and Local Studies.

Albert Porter's Quadrille Band

36 Information source and photograph – courtesy Rochdale Local Studies Centre.

Richard Snape's String Band

37 Information from Tony Snape, son of Leo Snape (band member).

James Titherington's String Band

38 Photograph – courtesy of Colne library.

Henry Wilson's Band

39 Information from the 'Dalesman Magazine' November 1950. The interview with Henry Wilson is by William R. Mitchell. (I Spoke to William Mitchell November 2013). Thanks to Nita Dewar (Long Preston) for alerting me to the article.

40 Extra information from George Carr of Long Preston, his mother was Kate Wilson, the pianist in the photograph and his grandfather was George Wilson, holding the double-bass (August 2011).

Matt. Worsley's Orchestra

41 Earlier photograph and details of band members, courtesy of Jim Lawrenson.
42 Photograph and background information from his grand-daughter Angie Livingstone September 2014.
43 Information from 'Brindle as I remember it' by Harold Baxendale.
44 Ed. Worsley, grandson September 2014.

Leyland Motors Orchestral Band

45 Photograph – courtesy of Leyland Library.
46 'Will it be fine do you think' – The story of Leyland Morris Dancers by Roy Smith.
47 Photograph – courtesy of Leyland Commercial Vehicle Museum, Leyland.

Herbert Whittaker's Ladies' Orchestra

48 Information from amounderness.co.uk

Alban Yates' String Band (Wheelton)

49 Information from Joyce Coulborn, daughter of Howard Roberts June 2010.
50 Information from Rex and Roy Marsden, sons of Alan Marsden. Roy was also a cornet player and drummer with various dance bands, including the Olympic Dance Band.
51 'Memories of old Withnell Fold' by Florence Scott – Countryside Publication 1988
52 'Brindle as I remember it' by Harold Baxendale.
53 'Brindle Parish Council Centenary' booklet by Ron Blackburn.
54 Arcadian Dance Band (Withnell) – information from Evan's brother, Jack Pilkington, Whittle-le-Woods, July 2010.

Brass Bands

55 Photograph and information about Rivington musicians – courtesy of Thomas Lowe.

East Lancashire Concertina Bands

56 Photograph – courtesy of Accrington Library.

East Lancashire Reed Bands

57 Photograph – courtesy of Clitheroe Library.
58 Photograph – courtesy of Accrington Library.

Cinema Orchestras / Horsfield's Orchestra

59 Archives from Greater Manchester Record Office.
60 Information – Jane Critchley's daughter, Audrey and husband Peter Hunter.

Harmonica Bands

61 Information and photograph – courtesy of Elan Murphy and Lucy Harwood.

Long Nights

62 Information and photograph – courtesy of Jim and Pat Bolton.

All newspaper references are from the *Preston Guardian*, unless otherwise stated.

Lancashire Libraries: particularly Chorley, Lancaster, Accrington, Fleetwood, St. Annes, Leyland, Clitheroe, Rawtenstall, Leyland and Darwen.
Wigan Library
Rochdale Library
Kendal Library
Horwich Library
Nineteenth-century British newspapers
British Newspaper Archive